The Basset Chronicles

June J. McInerney

Illustrated by Linda F. Uzelac

B'Seti Pup Publishing

First Edition

ISBN-13: 978-1466405561
ISBN-10: 1466405562
LCCN: 2011919631

DEDICATION

To those everywhere
who love and admire
Basset Hounds,
Most specially
to those who are fond of mine
and who supported me while I wrote this book:
Lin and Steve, Sister Peg and "Uncle" Dan,
Cathy, Fenn, Brian, Maria, and Michael,
Betty and Joe,
And, of course, thanks to
"Frankie," "FrankieB," and "Sebastian".

CONTENTS

ACKNOWLEDGMENTS

Cover portrait of "FrankieBernard"©2010
by Bookwalter Photographics, Carlise, PA

The "Biblical Years" stories are based upon various books of
The Life Application Bible: New Revised Standard Version©1989,
World Bible Publishers, Inc., Iowa Falls, Iowa

"Why Dogs Have Wet Noses" is loosely based up a "tail" from
What Do Dogs Know? by Stanley Coren and Janet Walker.
Published by Free Press ©1997

The poems in "Frankie Poetry" were originally published in
Spinach Water and *Exodus Ending*,
also by the author.

These stories could not have been written without the
assistance of both "Frankie" and "FrankieB", who, of course,
were able to tell me as I wrote them, each in his own way,
what really happened.

AUTHOR'S NOTE

This is primarily a work of fiction.
However, some of the characters and locations
are real or are based upon real people and places.
I have taken the liberty of ascribing fictional dialogue and
behavior to those people that are real, as well as augmenting
or changing the description of some of the real places
to suit the context of these stories.

PART I:

THE BIBLICAL YEARS

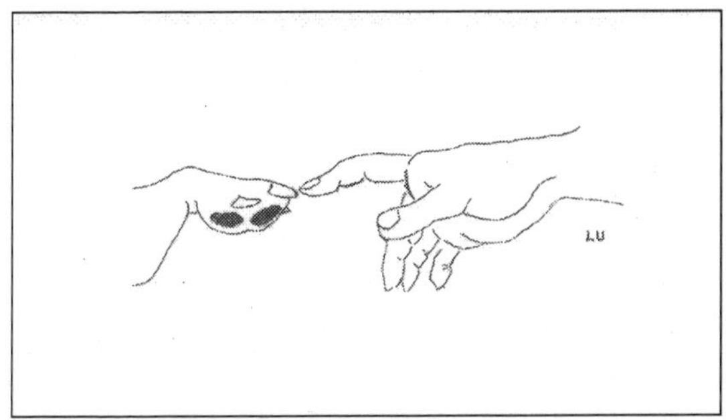

HOW BASSET HOUNDS WERE CREATED

Now, in the early part of the evening of the Sixth Day of Creation, God was sitting in his easy chair recliner, newly stuffed with goose-down, in front of a warm, crackling fire in his Cloud Den located on the lower Firmament level of Heaven. He had just completed making all the animals, including mankind, male and female alike did he make them, that dwell upon the Earth. It had been, by far, the longest day of Creation and He was really, really tired.

For, from the rising of the newly fashioned greater light of the Sun to its setting and the appearance of the lesser light of the Moon, God had been very busy. Eternally working non-stop, in turn He created just about every living creature of every kind, including the cattle and creeping things and wild animals, even spiders and snakes, and slippery, muddy worms. And when he saw that they were all lively and thriving and that it was Good, He made humankind in the image of Himself and then made the inhabitants of all the levels of Heaven to assist Him in maintaining the Creation.

That was the hardest part of His day, because there are nine types of Heavenly inhabitants, divided into three hierarchies of Choirs: Seraphim, Cherubim, and Thrones; Dominions, Powers, Virtues, and Mights; and Principalities, Archangels, and Angels, of which there is the littlest one, named Miniminuel. And each and every one of the types is quite different. So, as you can imagine it took Him a long time to create Heaven's residents, whom we now know as Angels.

It took God a longer time, almost an eternity, to create the first man and woman, combining all the best qualities of the heavenly Hosts to get Adam and Eve to look and sound and act just right. He had to be especially careful to give them just the right amount of free will so that they would choose to love, honor, and obey Him in all things as far as it was humanly possible.

In addition, He had to be careful about what all the living creatures were to eat; making sure it was not each other. So He made the Divine decision to allow them to feast on the plants and fine Garden greenery. Animals and humans alike were to have for food every plant yielding seed and every tree with seed in its fruit. That was especially hard, because as God created, He discovered that each and every creature had his or her own particular and peculiar tastes. The horse only ate oats and barley, the cows, grasses, and the fish, green plankton. Humans craved a variety of green vegetables and fresh salads, including olives and romaine lettuce. At the end of the Sixth Day, God felt more like a restauranteur than a Creator.

But, in the end, He saw that everything was, indeed, very Good. However creative He was, though, God was, indeed, very, very omnipotently tired.

God sighed heavily and deeply, sagging deeply into the soft, caressing folds of the chair, slowly sipping His foaming, fermented drink.

"Ah, yes, it all looks good. But such hard work. If I had only known how much trouble it would be to create mankind, to find the right kind of mate and companion, to feed him well...at least I don't have to worry about clothing them. Like the new lilies of the field, they need not worry, for I will provide.

"Ahhhh," He yawned. "Tomorrow is another day, the Seventh Day. From now on and all through that day, I shall rest." And having thus spoken, God settled Himself into the goose-feather filled pillows, muttering, "One of the best Creations I've done so far." Feeling that all was good, He smiled and instantly fell into a deep sleep, gently and peacefully snoring.

Down on earth, however, it was far less than peaceful. Commotion after the Creation reigned amidst the Trees of Knowledge and of Good and Evil in the middle of the Garden of Eden. For scurrying frightened and lost under the lush, low growing bushes, unable to find his path back to God, was Miniminuel, the littlest angel. All of Creation was quite new to this gentlest of souls and Eden, with all of its newness of life, was quite overwhelming to him. And so he sat, huddled between the lowest branches of the thickest mulberry bush, cowering and sorely afraid.

The newly created animals, of course, were upset. All animals, especially mammals, can smell human and angelic emotions, especially fear. And they certainly sensed the fear of the littlest angel. Because they were unable to see him, they, in turn, became afraid and began to trample upon the earth. The two new humans, Adam and Eve, were not aware, of course, of why the animals, the cattle, the oxen, the giraffes, the turtles, the elephants, the lions, and the tigers, and the bears—oh my—were beginning to stampede and so they, too, began to grouse and grumble and become afraid.

The lesser light rose high into the Heavens over the twinkling stars, glowing through the window of God's Cloud Den where He lay gently sleeping. But down on Earth, the animals snorted and hissed and stomped while

Adam and Eve began to complain about the noise. And God, of course, was totally oblivious to what was happening below. He snorted and snored and coughed, turning over on His side, causing large rumbles of thunder to roll and clap through the cumulous clouds, sparking and spewing lightning across the Garden. This frightened the animals even more, causing Adam and Eve to seek shelter from harm's way in the boughs of the Tree of Good and Evil, whose fruit, though forbidden, smelled absolutely temptingly luscious.

At the precise moment when Adam and Eve decided to hide from the animals, the Heavenly Hosts of Heaven gathered before God as He slept.

The four Major Archangels—Ariel, Raphael, Gabriel, and Michael—strode purposefully across the cirrus-shagged rug of the Cloud Den and stood as a phalanx at the feet of God, waiting for Him to awaken.

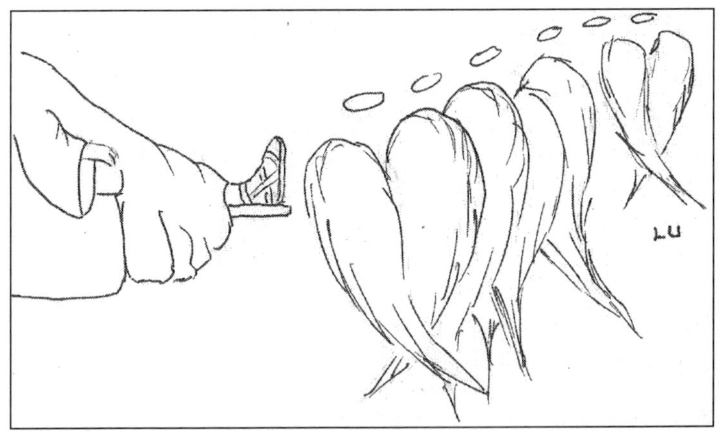

"I really don't think He will. He looks so peaceful in a very deep sleep," Ariel said, wrapping her wings around her shoulders.

"He just has to," Raphael said. "Our littlest angel, Miniminuel, is missing, and we need His Great Majesty's help to find him."

Gabriel bristled and ruffled his own wing feathers. "I've trained Mini well," he said. "He should be able to take care of himself."

"But he's the littlest and youngest. And, in our haste, we did leave him behind when we left the Garden of Eden amidst all those wild animals God created. He must be very frightened," Michael said. "We must wake God."

"But how?" Ariel asked.

"You just did!" God thundered, turning his wrath upon the phalanx of angels standing before Him. The very walls of the Cloud Den shook and rattled. "And I was having the most wonderful dream...I was walking in a lush garden with ripening tomatoes and green cucumbers and bright, red strawberries, talking with two men named Noah and Moses..."

"Oh, God!" Michael shouted, beside himself. "Enough with the reverie. Miniminuel is missing and we need Your help to find him."

"What?!" God exclaimed, jumping up and straightening his newly sewn ermine robes. "What have you done?"

"We didn't do anything," Ariel tried to explain. "When You had finished with The Creation and left, we tidied up the Garden and then summoned the Firmament Elevator to carry us back to Heaven. We thought he was close behind us, but as the doors closed, we realized he wasn't. And, well..."

"You left him there?" God asked, quite annoyed. "But he's so little and unarmed against the wild beasts..."

"That's what we thought," Michael asserted. "Which is why we came to You and had to wake You up. Sorry, God. Mea culpa."

"That's okay, my son," God said. "Let's see what we can do to get Miniminuel back up here."

He walked to the huge picture window that spanned the Firmament of Heaven and overlooked the tops of the trees that grew in the Garden of Eden. Beside it was a stellar telescope on an adjustable tripod. He swung it into place and adjusted the eyepiece to 120X strength, scanning the horizons of Earth.

The angels stood behind Him, anxiously waiting for the littlest angel to be found.

After a while, Ariel impatiently said, "Well, do You see anything?"

"Hold on," God said, still looking into the eyepiece, waving His hand behind His back to shoo Ariel away. "Not yet...wait, hold on. I think I've got something. Yes, there he is...under that mulberry bush. There, do you see?" He moved away to give Ariel a chance to look.

"Hey, everyone! There he is!

" Ariel exclaimed. "See?" Each of the Archangels, in turn, took a look into the telescope, watching as Miniminuel crouched and cowered, cornered by a lion, unable to make his escape.

Gabriel unsheathed his mighty, gleaming sword. "I will get him!" he shouted, running out the door towards the Firmament Elevator. "Hang on, my little friend. Help is on the way!"

When Miniminuel was safely back in the higher Firmament of Heaven and rested from his ordeal, having been rescued by Gabriel, he appeared before God to tell Him how the Archangel had scared the fiercely roaring lion away with his fiery sword and then carried him safely to the Elevator.

"Ah, yes, that was Good," God said. "Good of Gabriel. And now you are safe."

"Yes, I am," said Miniminuel. "But..."

"But?"

"But..." Miniminuel folded his wings neatly behind his back, as he had been taught to do in the presence of

God, and indicating a stool next to God's recliner, asked if he could sit down.

"Of course, my little son," God said. "What is on your mind?"

"Well," the littlest angel began. 'I know that You created Adam first, and then Eve out of his rib for his mate. But I think..." Miniminuel hesitated.

"Yes?"

"If I may..."

"Go on."

"I think," the angel said, shifting on the stool, "that they need, um, a companion."

"A companion?"

"Yes. Kind of what one would call a, um, pet?"

"A pet?" God mused. "What a novel idea."

"Well, yes. While I was lost under the bush, I overheard them talking and while they seemed happy enough, they were looking for someone, something to, well, raise together and cherish."

"I was planning children for them," God asserted.

"Yes, but until that time, God," Miniminuel countered, "a pet would fill the bill. And when the children do come, it could help them raise the kids. Teach them responsibility and all that…"

"What did you have in mind?"

"Well, something in the way of a dog."

"A dog?"

"Yes. A dog."

God thought about this for a long time, while the littlest angel sat preening wing feathers by His side. Finally, after what seemed eons, God said, "It's a strange name…dog. But…this is Good. Since you had the idea, Mini, I want you to form a committee of angels, one from each of the three choirs and the major Archangels—you will be the Chair-angel. Plan out what this 'pet' is to look like, and, if I agree that it would be suitable for Adam and Eve, I will add it to my Creation. Agreed?"

"Agreed!" said Miniminuel, quite pleased with himself. And he hurried off to form his committee.

When the hierarchy of Archangels heard of God's decision to have the littlest angel of the lowest rank of the inhabitants of Heaven head up the Committee to Create a Canine Companion for Adam and Eve, Raphael, Gabriel, Michael, and even Ariel (who was the most democratic and understanding of all the Archangels) bristled. Since their very inception, they always were to be assigned to head up all of the Heavenly committees, and were always put in charge of the biggest tasks and assignments. After all, this *was* the littlest, as well as the youngest, angel. What did he know? What experience did he have that they didn't that would make him their leader?

Miniminuel, as well, while pleased with his new assignment, was not so very sure himself he'd be up to the task of managing his superiors. But since he had great faith in God, and, it seemed, God had such great faith in him, he uncurled his wings, smoothed down their feathers, and proudly marched to the Heavenly Meeting Hall, where all the great decisions about the new Creation were to be made.

As they were all gathering in front of the wide oaken doors of the Angelic Conference Room in the Heavenly Meeting Hall, Raphael, Gabriel, Michael, and

Ariel in great cacophony, and all at once, related their ideas, advice, and suggestions to Miniminuel as to how he should run the meeting—what tasks he should assign each of the committee members, and how the "pet" should look, and how to present the Plan of a Creature Creation to God.

Miniminuel strutted to the doors and before he opened them, turned to the Archangels shouting and gesturing and advising him.

"Stop!" he said, dead in his tracks, his feet planted firmly on the tiled floor. "I have my own ideas. I have everything under control!"

"We'll see about that!" Raphael said, pushing the doors open and striding into the conference room before Miniminuel. He planted himself in the chair at the head of the table and was adjusting his wings when Ariel sat down in a seat along an edge of the table and said:

"Raphael, I know you are used to being in charge of everything angelic around here and are sometimes God's right hand, but this is Miniminuel's thing, now. That's his place to sit, not yours."

"Who says?"

"God says."

"Oh," said Raphael and as the littlest angel humbly walked into the room to take his place at the head of the committee, he meekly got up and moved to a corner chair at the other end of the room. To himself he thought: I'll be watching you. To Miniminuel he said:

"All yours, little guy. Let's see what you can do."

Since there were ten members of the committee, each representing the eight levels or ranks of the Inhabitants of Heaven, Miniminuel decided that each of them would suggest a trait that the new pet dog for Adam and Eve would have. When they were all assembled and seated, their wings comfortably adjusted around them, he proposed this to the Committee. Every member agreed.

"So far, so good," he said.

"Now, Raphael," he said, straining to see the Archangel at the far end of the room, smugly curled up in his wings. "You go first. What trait would you suggest?"

"Well, I am the Angel of Healing and Protection, you know. So, I propose that the new creature have long, white teeth and a big chest. We'll call that a brisket...so that he can bare his canines—pardon the pun—and growl and snarl and maul any predators, if need be. And he has to stand steadfastly and stalwartly on his feet to protect his new human companions."

"Good suggestion," the Chair-angel said. "Agreed?" he asked the rest of the Committee. No one demurred, so he moved on to Michael.

"The pet has to be loyal," the second Archangel said. "So, I, too, suggest he be loyal, resolute, dedicated, and persistent. To show that, his tail should be really long, with a large, white tip, that wags wildly when they greet him and stands erect when he is in the field, so that Adam and Eve can see him wherever he is and know that he is thinking about and with them all the time."

"Wait," interjected Ariel. "We're all saying, 'he' and 'him'. Are we all agreed that this pet—thing—should be male and why not, um, female?" She shook her feathered wings in such a way that the male Committee members sat straight up in their seats and dipped their haloes at her in what seemed like a newfound recognition.

"Good point, Ariel," Miniminuel said. "But for the first go-around of this 'draft' model, I think male at first. The female of breed will come later, you think?"

"Hmm, well, yes," Ariel said, preening even more. "Practice does make perfect!"

Miniminuel continued around the room, with each angel offering his trait in turn.

Metaton, the Angel of Length, offered a long, low-slung body and longevity of life so that the newly formed companion would be able to scamper under low bushes and also be with Adam and Eve for a long time. Camuel offered deep love and great eyesight in big, brown, watery eyes that would look both sad and appealing.

When it was Orofactel's turn, she sighed and took a long time to answer.

"Well," she said. "I was thinking about the ears. They would have to be very long and wide and wing-like. Simply because, and I am sure we will all agree, that we can't think of anything that doesn't exist without some semblance of wings—like we have." She stopped to brush the tops of hers and then continued.

"While God created Adam and Eve in His own Image, I would think that whatever we, the Angels, design to be created as the companion of mankind should carry a part of what we are—our wings. Besides, the long, wide ears could also be used not so much in hearing, but in scooping up scents on the ground into the dog's nose. A great sense of smell, a million times better than that of Adam's, will help the human in his hunting."

"What a great idea!" Ariel exclaimed. The rest of the group applauded loudly and long.

"Seems like we're all agreed on that one," Miniminuel said. "Say, is anyone taking this all down?"

"I am," boasted Camuel, showing the notes and sketches he was making.

"Great job," the Chair-angel said. "Who's next?"

As the rest of the afternoon wore on, the rest of the Committee offered the remaining traits. Gabriel added a really long snout with a great sense of smell to compliment Orofactel's ears. Uriel gave a singing, baying, howling voice along with the deep brisket. Sandalphon gave short, stubby legs and large, wide paws so that he could stand squarely on them and not lose his balance when he ran. Ariel offered her mercy and gentleness with a soft, smooth coat of fur. And, lastly, Atheniel gave the gift of being a great, skilled hunter.

After everyone else was finished, and everyone agreed to the choices, Miniminuel offered his.

"He should be honest and forthright. Maybe a bit stubborn, with a mind of his own, but kind and honest just the same. And a good cuddler."

Camuel jotted all of the traits down, with their descriptions, and drafted a plan which included not only text, but a sketch and creation details. When it was completed, he presented it to Miniminuel who, in turn, presented it to the rest of the Committee to Create a Canine Companion for Adam and Eve.

The last thing to decide was what to call the newest member of the animal kingdom. Because he was so low to the ground, they settled on calling it a Basset hound; "basset" meaning "settled low" and "hound" meaning, well, "hunter".

"Are we ready for our final vote?" the Chair-angel asked, scanning the room with his tiny eyes.

Reluctantly impressed by what he had seen, Raphael was the first to raise his right wing to say, "Aye! I agree!" The rest of the Angels and Archangels fluttered their wings and followed suit. "Aye! Aye! Yes, yes, and I agree wholeheartedly!" Everyone concurred.

"It's unanimous!" Miniminuel declared. "Tomorrow we will bring our Plan to God!"

The next day, on the Eighth Day of Creation, Miniminuel, Raphael, Michael, and Ariel appeared before God, who was once again supine in His great recliner in His Cloud Den, with His feet up, pointing His soles to the Garden of Eden, sipping a brewsky, and watching a Celestial League baseball game on His wide-screen HDTV. The Cherubim Haloes were losing to the Seraphim Harps, 7 to 9, in the bottom of the eighth inning, and He was getting a bit agitated.

"Yes, what is it now?!" He shouted at the door, when Raphael softly rapped on it.

"Sorry to disturb You, Great Father," Miniminuel whispered as he pushed open the door, but You did say that when my, er, our Committee completed its tasks, we were to immediately come to You. "

"And, so, I did, little one," God said, reaching for the remote and pressing Mute. "It's a close, but disappointing game. This, it seems, is more important," seeing the huge, red and white folder Miniminuel was carrying.

"Okay," God said. "Let's see what you got."

God perused the plan and the sketches very carefully, and for a long time. He pondered the creation details, then turned the sketches this way and that to get a better idea of what the Committee to Create a Canine Companion for Adam and Eve was proposing.

"Hmmm," He finally said, taking another sip of his brewsky. He eyed the muted HDTV. The Haloes were still losing in the top of the ninth. "Bummer," He whispered under His breath, then turned off the TV. "Better luck next time."

God waved the Angels and Archangels to the other side of the room to make space in the center of the floor of his Cloud Den. He spread His arms wide to the Universe and said, "Let there be this Basset Hound!" And, lo, in the middle of the Den suddenly appeared a small hound, with very long ears, two droopy too-sad eyes, four very big paws, a very long, white-tipped tail, a long snout, and a very soft, velvety coat of dark reddish-brown fur, mixed with large patches of gleaming white on his back, across one shoulder, and on his plump belly.

And this is what he looked like:

God stared at the Basset puppy for a long time, as the puppy looked around at his new surroundings, not sure where he was or whom he was with. He cringed on a corner of the carpet and embarrassingly, out of fright and uncertainty, stained it.

"Ah, geez," Miniminuel said, "you're not supposed to do that..."

"It's okay," Michael said. "He's not trained yet. Too new to do anything else. You'd be frightened, too, if your first sight in life was that of God."

The Very Omnipotent Being continued to stare at the Basset. He didn't say anything. The Angels stood very still in anticipation, for God did not say, "And it was Good," as He normally does after making something. Instead, He "hmmmed" and "hawed" and stroked His long, white beard. Finally, he said:

"Very interesting. You all seemed to have captured the best parts of all dogs, if ever I was to create them. He's, um, well quite funny looking. However, I have been thinking about starting out with the basic grey Wolf and letting the species evolve from there."

Having made a decision, He raised His right hand and pointed His finger at the little puppy sniffing the cirrus-shag rug, about to erase what He had just made."No! God, no!" shouted Miniminuel. "Please don't destroy what You've just created. I beg of You. I pray to You...Don't!"

"And why not, Little Angel?"

"Because that is the first of Your Ordinal Rules, remember? Thou shalt not destroy what Thou hast created..."

"...unless it is justly deserved," Gabriel said. "Miniminuel is right. No destruction."

The Basset, sensing how ominous it was to have the Omnipotent Finger pointing at him, quivered in fright, as if he knew that his short, brief existence was tenuous at best—in very grave danger.

Michael said, "Look at him. He's just a naïve little puppy. What has he done to deserve Your wrath to be destroyed just because he may be 'funny looking'?"

"Well, I, um, I mean to say..." God sputtered, lowering His arm. "Maybe you do have a point."

"I know, I know!" Ariel jumped up and down to be noticed. "Let's not be so hasty. Let's let Adam and Eve decide."

God thought about this. "Well," He mused, "since he is to be their companion, that may be the wisest action to do here. Proceed."

"Yes!" Miniminuel and Ariel yelled together, jauntily giving each other a mighty high-five with the tips of their wings.

Sensing that he was saved by God, the puppy wagged his long, white-tipped tail in delight. Without thinking and definitely without warning, he bounded up onto God's lap, spilling His drink all over His ermine robe, planted his large, front paws squarely upon His chest, and joyously licked His face, slobbering all over God's nose and mouth.

It was indeed a funny sight and the Angels did indeed laugh, rollicking the very Firmament of Heaven until God pushed the Basset Hound puppy off His chest, stood up, brushed puppy hair off his robes with His hands, and with a great, blue bandana, wiped puppy spittle from His mouth.

"That is quite enough," God said. "Take him away!"

And, so, they did.

Raphael picked up the puppy and gathered him into his protective arms. He carried him to the Firmament of Heaven Elevator that connected the first Level with the Garden of Eden.

Adam was noshing on the last part of a peach and gnawing on the pit by the Waterfall of Eden, swishing his feet in the pond formed at its base, when he heard a great fluttering of wings and tiny, high-pitched yips. He looked up and saw four angels—one the tiniest speck with wings he had ever seen—drifting down toward him.

"Hello, Adam," Gabriel said. "How are you doing? We've got something for you."

"It's been two or more days since you've been earthed by God out of mud and rock, so we thought you'd like a belated birth, er, earth day present," Raphael said, placing the puppy beside Adam on the grass. Immediately, curious creature that he was, the little hound began sniffing at the peach.

"Not for you," Adam said, moving the mostly eaten peach to his other hand, away from the prying nose. "He's rather funny looking, isn't he? And, he is a 'he', isn't he?"

"Funny looking. Huh. That's just what God said," Ariel remembered. "And yes, he is a hymn, er, a him."

Adam examined the puppy very carefully before asking, "What does he do?"

"Do?" asked Miniminuel.

"Purpose?" queried Adam. "His ears are too long, his legs too short, his tail too tall, and his paws too big. And, in case you haven't noticed, he is really, really short."

"Vertically challenged," said Ariel.

"Yes, well…still."

"He is to be your companion," Raphael said.

"But I have Eve," Adam stated.

Just then, as if on cue, Eve walked out of the forest behind the Waterfall of Eden, cradling a large, red Macintosh apple in her left hand. She was about to take a bite out of it when she caught sight of the Basset puppy sitting expectantly by Adam's rib.

"Good morning, Madam," to Eve said Adam.

"Good morning, Sir," to him said she.

"What have we here?" she inquired, gesturing to the puppy at his side. "And why are all these angels here? Have we done something wrong already?"

"Oh, no, dear, nothing like that," Adam said. "They've come to give us this." He picked up the little hound and held it out to her.

Gabriel glared at the apple in Eve's hand.

"What do you have there?" he asked.

"What? Oh, this?" she responded, looking at the apple in her hand , then tossing it into the woods. "It is nothing. But this, this…" she said taking the Basset Hound puppy into her arms, "is something." Sensing unconditional love and maternal warmth, he instantly pressed his dry nose into the curve between her long, white neck and alabaster shoulders. He began to chortle softly.

"Why, he's just adorable," she cooed. To Adam she asked, "May we keep him?"

"Of course!" he said. "Apparently, he's a gift from the angels on the belated occasion of our Creation Day. Isn't that right?" he asked, turning to the angels.

"Yes, yes, the Basset is yours," they sang in unison, forming a choir in front of Adam and Eve, and singing a capella. "To raise and love, and take care of. Protect him always and he will soon grow to be your cherished companion!"

"He is a Basset Hound," Miniminuel explained. "Basset means 'low to the ground'."

"He certainly is," Adam said, watching the hound leap from Eve's arms and scamper under the bushes after a rabbit. "What shall we call him?" he asked her.

"Well, he is endearing..."

"We've already named one of the Cervidae 'deer', dear."

"And, so, we did. Well, then, he is cute," Eve tried again.

"Well...we did call the furry guinea pig an 'Agouti', didn't we?"

"Hmmm. Well...he's, um, he's..."

"He was designed to be loyal, faithful, forthright, open, truthful, outspoken, steadfast, above-board, and, above all, honest," Miniminuel proposed.

"Is that so? Adam said, finishing the last of his peach and scrunching the pit into the ground beside him.

"Then we shall call him 'Frank'!" Adam and Eve both decided at the same time.

The angels agreed that that was the best name for the Basset Hound. God looked down from Heaven through His telescope and saw that it was Good.

And ever since then, the Basset Hound has been the best and most lovable companion of men and women of all ages.

And so that's how Basset Hounds were created.

And that's how they are still to this day.

Except, of course, for having wet, not dry, noses.

The next story in these chronicles relates how that happened.

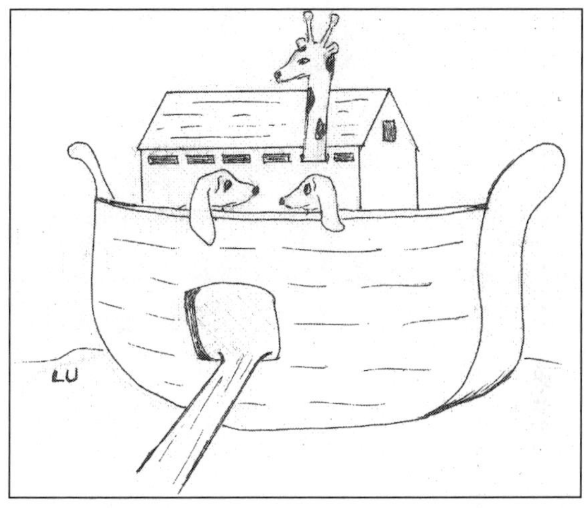

WHY DOGS HAVE WET NOSES

When Noah built the Ark and gathered the animals in, two by two, he brought in a brace (the hunting word for a pair) of Basset Hounds. These were by far not the first dogs ever created by God, but they were the most interesting, having been, you see, first designed by a committee of the lesser Angels. But that is another story in the beginning of these *Chronicles*. Noah was quite partial to Basset hounds, having had a few of them himself in his earlier childhood. So, when it came time to decide which breeds were to go and which were to stay, he chose two Bassets to board the huge boat.

What is most important to this story is that this brace of Bassets, Frankie and Judy, were the most industrious and conscientious of all the Ark animals. From their first day of creation, hounds were never the kind of dog that just lounged around waiting for their dinner and a few bones to be tossed to them. Oh, no. They were the kind of dog that worked for their keep, often even singing for their supper, howling the vowels of their human companions' favorite psalms. Can't you just imagine the Twenty-third Psalm sung by a deep-throated Basset?

"The Looooo-wooo-rd is my shep-woooooo-eeeeeerd. I shall-wooo-ooooooooo not wa-oooooo-nt."

Quite melodic, don't you think?

Anyway, Frankie and Judy were not going to take a free ride from Noah without showing their deep appreciation for all his endeavors to save his family and the best of humanity's companions. So, they struck up a bargain with him. It was to be, you might say "their right of passage". And it was this: They would patrol the big Ark every night and every morning, making sure that all was well with all of the passengers that dwelled therein the various rooms, sections, and stalls.

They promised to faithfully keep watch over all the seven pairs of the clean animals, and each pair of all the unclean animals, not to mention the seven pairs of each of the many species of birds that flew freely around the Ark's roof and rafters. From the very first raindrop, when God sealed the big wooden doors of the Ark, Frankie and Judy took their tasks very seriously and did them quite assiduously.

It was, as you can imagine, a daunting prospect, for the Ark was not just a little dingy. No, it was bigger than that. It was not just a large boat or a super-sized ship. It was actually humongous! Colossally gigantic. A really immense ship; bigger than any one you could ever imagine. It was as long as from here to your best friend's house across town, as wide as the Grand Canyon, and twice as tall as five Sequoia redwood trees standing end-to-end one on top of each other. Now, that's a **BIG** boat. No wonder it took Noah and his sons so long to build it.

Frankie and Judy patrolled every inch of the floating animal kingdom. Each and every morning they would arise bright and early from their soft straw Basset beds in the canine kennel corner of one of the Ark's midsections, where all the four-footed mammals were boarded, and begin their audit of the Ark.

They sniffed every plank of the cypress wood, trudging from the very bottom keel to the tall, massive bridge way up top where Noah and Shem captained and steered the ship through the raging storm and coursing waters. It took them a long time. As you know, Bassets have very short, stocky, but cute, legs and they take four times as many steps as we do to walk the same distance. So, by lunchtime, they were only half way through with their watch and would often stop amidships to eat with the sheep, goats, cows, and other bovine corralled in the middle stalls.

Frankie, you see, was very partial to yogurt and New York sharp cheddar cheese, of which, of course, that section had more than enough to share. And so he would linger there the longest, hoping to savor a few choice tidbits. And each visit, his hopes were fulfilled. For as every hound learns at a very young age, if you sit and stare at something long enough, you will get it. So, each day, he would sit and stare at a hunk of cheese or a cup of yogurt until one of the cows, tired of Frankie begging, threw him a piece of cheddar or a soupspoon full of yogurt.

And so, every afternoon after lunch, they would finish their patrol by ambling along the outside walls of the interior top decks, checking out the birds and the bees in the broad-beamed rafters, and eventually hiked up the wide gangplank to the bridge to report their findings to Noah.

For the first few days of what was to be a little more than forty days and forty nights of absolutely drenching rain, every thing and every being seemed to be fine. As Frankie did the majority of the sniffing and searching, Judy chatted amiably with each pair of animals they passed, asking, "Do you have everything you need? Is the journey smooth enough for you? Are you comfortable? Enough straw, fodder, and grain to eat?" Often she would check to make sure that no one was seasick. If any one was, she offered her special remedy for the woo-sies—a dash of sugar on a slice of the bitterest lemon she could sniff out, sprinkled with a dash of crushed mustard seed.

Well, in the beginning, the voyage all seemed to be going very smoothly, according to God's plan.

But one day down in the bowels of the Ark, along the outer edge of the cypress-hewn keel, Frankie thought he sniffed a damp scent.

"Cowoooo-woo-wooo wouldn't be," he howled as softly as he was able, loud enough to alert Judy but quiet enough so as not to alarm any of the larger hippopotami and elephants that were living down there.

Judy padded softly over to him, sniffing in the same direction as Frankie's smooth, round, black nose. In those days, you realize, dog and hound noses were smooth, without side notches, and as dry as crinkled sandpaper. Frankie sniffed again, this time taking hard, short snorts of air that whistled through his leathery nostrils like a baby breathing through a wooden fife.

"Oo-wooo-wooo-wet!" he howled again. "There, Judy, in one of those port planks that separate the raging waters from the safe, dry land banks built for the big mastodons and hippos."

Judy sniffed and sighted along the path of Frankie's pointing paw.

"There, Judy. Can you smell it?"

Judy sidled her long back next to Frankie's and whispered, "Yes, I can. It's a small hole, and water is slowly dripping from it. Oh, my!"

And sure enough, if you looked close enough, there was a hole in the plank, no bigger than the circle you can make with your thumb and forefinger, which is about the exact size of Frankie's nose.

"Wooo-wooo-wa-oooo-ter is leaking inside the Ark," Frankie snorted. "I suggested they reinforce the keel with oak, but noo-ooooo-oooo, Noah had to use the same cheap cypress wood with which they built the rest of this bucket of bilge, and now it's sprung a leak!"

"No use yelping over bad bark, Basset," Judy chided. "Best to decide what we're going to do about it now. By the time we get up to Noah and Shem, the raging waters will have built up, burst through, and basically have flooded the Ark, drowning all of us and the best of mankind, as well."

"So much for us," Frankie yelped, circling around his tail and pawing the keel boards so that he could comfortably lie down and think.

"Unless, unless…" he sighed, settling into a curl, his muzzle resting on a paw, as he tried to figure it all out.

"What are you thinking?" Judy quizzed, her eyebrows twitching in expectation. She knew full well that her lifelong mate had a plan. She had such great faith that he always did.

"Well, no use the two of us going the distance from here up to the bridge. Judy, you go and sound the alarm and I'll wait here for you to bring Noah and Shem. Remind Shem to bring his tar paper and hammer and pieces of wood to fix the leak."

"And what will you be doing in the meantime, might I ask?" Judy woofed.

"Plugging this darn hole with my nose."

Frankie got up from his curl, snuffled, and softly padded over to the keel hole. He snorted and then pushed his dry snout into the fissure where, sure enough, it was the perfect fit. His nose crammed into the leak so snugly, it stopped each and every little drip and drop of water on the outside of the Ark from dripping and dropping into the inside.

"Hurrumphyinmyupmmmph," he muffled, as Judy paddy-pawed as quickly as her stubby little legs could carry her over the single keel. In those days double hulls and keels for freighters and tanker ships had not yet been invented. Judy wriggled her way up the first step of stairs leading up to the bridge, as Frankie sat upon his short haunches, his nose stuck in place sniffing the watery world of the oceans beyond the Ark.

Now, Frankie knew it would take Judy the best part of the morning, almost well into lunch, to go the distance to where Noah and Shem were. He was fully prepared to have his nose stuck where it didn't belong for a long time, but was not prepared for the icy, cold, wet outside waters that battered against its leathery tip as the Ark plied its way through God's deluge of wrath against evil humanity.

Frankie, stubborn as he was to stick it out, was sorely tempted, at one point, to pop his nose right back out of the hole and have the waters flood the Ark, just to have it warm and dry once more. But, being the sort of hound he was, at the very last moment he decided against it. And so, for what seemed like days, but was really only hours, Frankie sat and stood and sat again with his snout stuck in the small crater, damming up the waters. He silently and stoically shivered with the icy cold dampness that traveled from his nose down to the very white tippy-tip of his hound tail.

Meanwhile, Judy bounded up stairs, across planks, down decks, through amidships, skipping lunch, until hours later, she panted her way wearily into the bridge where Noah was expertly navigating.

"Woof, wooof. Woof, wooooooof, woof, woof woof, woof," she said.

"Now, what's that you say?" Noah bent down to Judy to best hear her story, translating her barks and howls into the early Ancient Hebrew dialect that was spoken during those times.

Now, you know God picked Noah to save the animals because not only was he a godly and righteous man, but also because he was the only one on the earth at the time of the Great Flood who, like our modern day Dr. Doolittle, could talk to the animals. As a matter of fact, Dr. Doolittle is a direct descendant of Noah, and much of the same animal languages we speak today were spoken back then.

"A leak? In my keel!?" Noah thundered. "It just can't be!"

"Woof, wooof, arf, woof, yelp, woof woof woof," Judy continued.

"And you say Frankie has his nose where? Oh, my!" Noah cried. "Shem, bring your hammer and tar paper and a piece of cypress wood about the same size as this circle [**O**] made with my thumb and forefinger, which, I bet, is probably about the same size as Frankie's nose, and follow me."

He quickly ushered Judy out of the bridge and down the wide gangplank.

"Ham, you steer," he commanded his second son, while Shem bustled about, gathering his tools and falling down the stairs behind his father.

It took Judy longer to get back to Frankie because Noah, despite the distress and danger of having the Ark sink, had to occasionally stop and speak to a pair of giraffe here—"So, how is the weather up there? Still raining? Ah, I thought so."—a pair of turtles there—a flock of birds wherever—"And how is your new brood today? No, please don't be frightened. Nothing will harm you. Come out of your shell and talk to me." And so on, stopping at every third or fourth stall or room or section of each of the many Ark decks and levels until finally, in the early evening, they slid down the last ladder to the very bottom keel.

"Oh, my word and stars!" Noah exclaimed as he tugged his long beard and crawled out of sight into the port darkness where poor Frankie was now exhausted, half standing, half stooping his long, broad back to keep his nose from slipping out of the leaking hole. By now, a few drops of water were beginning to sneak by, dribbling down his long ears and drenching the silken fur on the front of Frankie's neck and upper chest.

His front paws were steeping in an icy puddle. Every so often, he would gingerly pick one up and try to shake excess water from it. But it was no use. Just as soon as he shook a paw, he had to plop it back into the puddle again to lift and shake the other.

"Oh, my word and stars!" Noah cried again. "Quickly, Shem, undo this dog and patch up that hole!"

And so Shem did, plucking Frankie's nose gingerly from the leak with a loud "Knowck-pop!" and quickly sealed up the hole with tar paper and wood.

"Wooooooooof!" Frankie howled in pain.

"Oh, dear! Oh, my!" Noah said, "What a great hound you are! And what a really wet nose you now have!" He patted Frankie's long damp ears and allowed him to lick his cheek. For, you see, Frankie was so grateful for being rescued, giving no thought to the brave deed he just did to save the Ark and all its inhabitants, he just wanted to thank Noah for saving him from certain drowning.

Judy danced for joy and when the hole was repaired and everyone on the Ark was assured that all was again well with their journey, she led Frankie back to their quarters in the canine corner of the kennel for four-legged mammals.

"Your nose is still wet and cold," she smiled, circling around him seven times to make a warm nest of straw around them.

"And I s-s-s-s-s-shiver- suspect it will be for a long time," Frankie said, unsuccessfully trying to snuffle the sneeze building in his snout. "Ka-woooo-woooo-woooo-kaaa-choo!"

"God bless you!" Judy said.

And as it so happened, when the Ark finally landed on a dry patch of earth, He did.

When the rains stopped and the waters receded after one hundred and fifty days, the Ark finally settled onto the land the raven had found. The black bird had vowed to succeed in his efforts because, you see, he would enter the Ark, as he put it, "Nevermore!"

Noah and his sons and wife and his sons' wives planted a great vineyard and built an altar to the Lord to give thanks for saving his family and all the animals. In return, God showed his own good faith by painting a huge multi-colored rainbow onto the pale blue palette of the sky.

One early evening, God came down from heaven to visit with Noah.

"That was a good thing you did, Noah," God said, "saving the animals and the best of mankind for me."

"Ah, it was almost nothing," Noah shyly smiled, veiling his eyes and trying not to look into the face of the Lord. "But it was Frankie who really saved the day."

"Frankie, the Basset hound?" God asked, knowing full well the whole story, but also knowing how much Noah loved to tell a tale. He listened with infinite patience as the Ark's captain related all that had happened and how Frankie sat and stood and stooped and stayed and shivered with his nose up a virtual creek for almost nine hours to stave off a sinking ship while Judy ran for help.

"Well," God said, beckoning Frankie to His side and beginning to stroke one of his silken ears, "I bet the pot of gold at the end of this rainbow that your nose is still wet."

"And notched, too," Frankie wailed, pointing his paw to where the sides of his snout had been cut and creased by the sharp wooden edges of the hole. "These will never go away."

"Nor shall your wet muzzle, my blessed friend," God replied. "For from this day forth to the end of all days, all dogs and hounds shall have wet noses as a badge of honor and for all of humankind to remember your bravery in saving the Ark and all its inhabitants."

And so it was. And so it is now.

And that is really why dogs have wet noses.

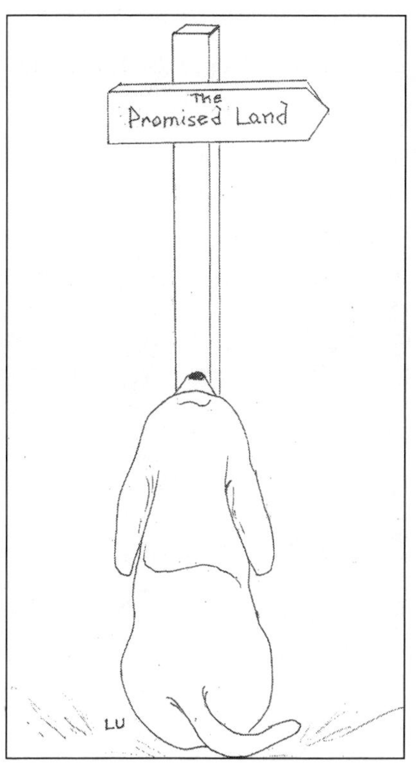

MOSES SUPPOSES

On the last night of the first occasion that we now know as Passover, FrankieA sat expectedly at the feet of Moses, who was seated at the long, rough-hewn wooden table eating and talking with his bother, Aaron. The black, tan, and white Basset Hound occasionally nudged Moses' knee, begging for a few bits of the unleavened bread hastily baked by Moses' sister, Miriam, or at least a small, savvy morsel from the roast of lamb.

"Not now, hound," Moses said. "I'm in the midst of something." He put down his fork, stood up, and rapped his long staff made of gopher wood on the tabletop. When he had everyone's attention, he cleared his throat and addressed the crowded room. It was filled to the low rafters with his family: his wife, Aaron's wife and many children, Miriam and her husband and children, Joseph the Ammonite, and various neighbors and close friends.

"Listen, my family and friends," Moses said. "Tomorrow morning, we will finally escape our slavery under Pharaoh. We will start our long journey through the wilderness to the Promised Land."

"How will we go, oh leader?" Joseph asked, scratching his long, white beard.

"We will walk, of course," Moses replied.

FrankieA's ears perked up when he heard "walk". He bounded to the door, scratching a side of the jamb with his forepaw.

"No, no, silly hound," Aaron said, pulling Frankie back from the door to a corner of the room. "He means we'll walk tomorrow. Tonight is not safe for beast nor man to be out."

FrankieA slinked back to Moses' side, and lay down with his long snout resting bashfully on his forepaws stretched in front of him.

"It will be a long, arduous trek, lasting many, many days," Moses continued. "We have been tasked by God to find the Promised Land and settle there."

"How long?" someone from the back of the room asked.

"I am not sure," Moses said. "I suppose quite a while."

"Longer than a month?" another neighbor queried?

"Perhaps longer than that?"

"Many months, Moses," Joseph mused. "I suspect the Promised Land is quite far away, over the river, through the desert, on the other side of the mountains. It will take us..."

"I suppose," Moses said wearily, cutting Joseph off.

Miriam, who was drying wooden bowls and plates after washing them in a large basin by the fire, asked, "What do we bring to last us on such a long journey for such a long time?"

"Surely God will provide for us," Zipporah, Moses' wife stated. "He got us through the seven plagues—surely he will get us through the arid desert."

Moses stroked his brown beard, speckled with grey. "I suppose he will, my wife. But we must also provide for ourselves. Aaron will take care of the details: what to pack, how much food we must take, when we are to leave."

"Early," Aaron said. "At the first crack of dawn before Pharaoh and his armies know we are even gone. Here's what we need to bring." He took a long papyrus scroll from the folds of his woolen tunic and unrolled it, slowly reading out each item listed on it. "Enough unleavened bread to last two months; two changes of clothing; an extra pair of sabots; hats to protect us from the glaring sun; all our cattle, sheep, goats, and whatever hens and chicks we can find; jugs of water packed in straw on carts to keep it cool—but we're only to use that sparingly; wine, dates, figs..." The list went on almost endlessly until FrankieA pushed his way through the crowd and jumped up on Aaron, firmly planting massive hound paws on his chest. He growled gently, as if to say, "You left me out. Don't I get to go, too?"

"And, yes, of course, we bring our beloved pets, including you, too, FrankieA." Aaron gently stroked the back of FrankieA's head. "Go lie down now, big fella, you'll need your rest for the long walk ahead of us."

The dog ambled over to the hearth and curled up in a neat, tidy ball on his rattan bed by the fire.

With that, everyone in the room set about finishing their dinner and helping Zipporah and Miriam clean up the remainder of the dinner dishes. Then they all began to pack what meager possessions they had in rustic sacks and wicker baskets woven from reeds of papyrus. Then they set about gathering everything on Aaron's list.

Moses retreated to his pallet by the door and sat, watching his family and friends work industriously, while he contemplated the days before him.

The next morning, before the sun even had a chance to peek over the desert sands, FrankieA was up howling, awakening Moses and Aaron and Miriam and Zipporah to start the day and their long walk. For there is nothing FrankieA, or any other Basset Hound for that matter, loves more than a good long walk with his companions. Well, maybe he likes a tasty treat now and then just a tiny bit better, but a long walk simply takes the cake.

"Alright, alright!" exclaimed Aaron, brushing the hound away. "Go wake up Moses."

"I'm already up, my brother. And so, it seems, is everyone else."

In the dim light of dawn, Moses and Aaron could see the bustling activity in the room. People were finishing their last minute packing and loading the many carts lined up outside facing east. When all was ready, Joseph the Ammonite handed Moses his long, gnarled staff and led him to the front of the crowd, eager to start their journey.

"Okay, everyone? Ready?" Moses asked, raising his staff above his head. FrankieA rushed to his side and with a mighty "Let's go!" from Moses, howled and yipped and bayed, bounding off into the fields towards the Red Sea.

"Well," Moses said, taking his first steps towards freedom and the Promised Land. "I am not sure where we are going, but I suppose at least we are on our way."

That afternoon, when the long line of travelers reached the shores of the river that separated Egypt from the Wilderness of Shur, Moses and Aaron looked back from whence they came and saw a huge cloud dust rising on the horizon behind them.

"It's Pharaoh and his gang," Aaron said. "He'll catch up to us in just a bit if we don't do something real soon, Moses."

Moses watched the looming cloud, then turned to the arm of the Red Sea stretched out before him and the multitude. then turned back to the advancing Egyptian army.

"Moses?" Aaron asked. "What do we do?"

"Not sure," Moses slowly said. "The river is wide, I am not sure we can go o'er..."

"Then, perhaps, we should try to go through it," Joseph the Ammonite said, walking slowly up to Moses' side. "Look!" he said, pointing to FrankieA running lickety-split toward the water where, standing tall on the bank, an Angel spread and fluttered his massive wings.

The masses began to express great fear.

"We'll be trampled by the horses of Pharaoh's army!" some screamed. "We'll be whipped by the angels and drowned in the sea!" others yelled. "Do something, Moses!" they all shouted, "or we'll die before we even have a chance to see the Promised Land, let alone live in it."

"Yes, Moses," Aaron said, shaking his brother's shoulder. "Do something!"

FrankieA raced back from the Angel to Moses, nipping and tugging at the bottom of Moses' robe, pulling him toward the shore, the very edge of the rushing waters.

"Rufff-ara-affffff! Rufff-ara-affffff!" the hound barked.

"Well, I suppose," Moses said, nodding tentatively to the Angel, "you're from God, aren't you?"

The Angel nodded, fluttered his wings once more, nodded again, and then floated past Moses and the multitude to hover between them and the advancing hordes of Pharaoh.

"Sent to save us," Moses said, watching the Angel.

"At least to help us save ourselves," Aaron said.

"Rufff-ara-affffff! Rufff-ara-affffff!" FrankieA barked again.

"Not now, hound!" Moses said. "I am in the middle of something. "

Zipporah, laden with baskets of food and a sack of clothing, walked to her husband's side.

"Maybe he's trying to tell you something," she said.

"I suppose," Moses said. "But what?"

"Sounds to me like he's trying to say, 'Raise your staff'."

Moses looked fondly at his wife, squeezed her arm, then said, "Of course." He stood at the edge of the

Red Sea and raised his long staff over his head. His people stopped yelling and screaming and stood in quivering silence, waiting to see what Moses would do next.

"Watch this," he said. And, arcing his staff in a slow sweep, he stretched it across the waters, and yelled, "In the name of God, part!"

And the waters did.

FrankieA was the first to bound onto the path of the river bottom that sluiced through the narrow channel that was formed by the walls of the parting Red Sea. Halfway across he howled and barked back to Moses, almost as astonished as the rest of the crowd, to follow him. Moses took a few tentative steps down the bank and into the corridor, then he turned to the multitude. In back, the Angel was beating off the army, urging the stragglers to keep up with the crowd slowly moving forward toward Moses. Aaron leaped off the bank to stand beside his brother.

"Come on, folks!" he shouted. "Follow us! We don't have all day!"

"I suppose that's for sure," Moses said, holding his staff high over his head, curbing the walls of water at bay. "I am not sure how much longer I can keep this up."

The ex-slaves of Egypt hurriedly rushed forward and poured through the parted Red Sea, following Moses and Aaron following FrankieA to the far shore of Shur. When they were all safely across, Moses stood on the bank and faced the Angel, who was luring Pharaoh and his army to the opposite side of the sea. Still holding his staff high, he waited until all the Egyptians were in the corridor.

Then the Angel turned to Moses and with a shimmer of his massive wings rose up into the sky. He nodded his head and Moses brought his staff down, striking the ground beside him.

The walls of the water crashed back together, sealing back together the fragmented Red Sea. The corridor and the bottom of the Red Sea disappeared. And so did Pharaoh and his army.

There was great rejoicing among Moses and his people. Miriam played her tambourine and sang and danced with Aaron and their children. Zipporah pounded her tambour and marched with Moses and

FrankieA through the crowd, accepting congratulatory hand slaps and chanting hymns of praise to both Moses and God.

"You did it, Moses!' they all said. "You saved us!"

"I suppose," Moses said. "But it was really God and His Angel and…tooo-wheet, tooo-wheet," he whistled. The black, tan, and white hound ran gleefully to his side. "…this little fellow here who told me to raise my staff! Thank you, FrankieA. Good job!" he said, patting the dog's side and scratching behind FrankeA's long, silken ears. "Good job!"

The next morning, after a long night of rejoicing, the Israelites (for that was what they began to call themselves, being, as they said, the "chosen ones of God") set out to cross the Wilderness of Shur. Shur was a harsh and unforgiving land, made up of parched rocks and hot, arid desert, without a plant, tree, or shrub in sight to hunker under for shade. For three days and nights, they marched over the powdery sand that crept into their sabots to nestle irritably between their toes and flaked unmercifully into their ears, eyes, and hair. There seemed to be no end or relief in sight except for the jugs of water packed in straw on the carts and the prospect in the far, distant future of a Promised Land.

On the evening of the third day, Aaron came to Moses, who was sitting with Zipporah, lazily brushing the sand off of FrankieA, and said, "My brother, we have a problem."

"What is it now?" Moses asked. "Have you found another sea for me to part?"

"Exactly the opposite," Aaron said. "We have run out of water."

"What? What happened to all those jugs of water we're carting?"

"All gone," Aaron sighed. "This land we're crossing is so hot and dry, that we drank more than we should have to keep hydrated. We should have brought more, but...well, the people are starting to complain of great thirst."

"I suppose," Moses said, getting up and dusting off his robe, "you'll want me to do something?"

"Yes, Moses, if you would."

"As if leading two million people out of Egypt, through the Red Sea, and over the desert of the Wilderness of Shur wasn't enough," Moses sighed, and walked away from Aaron toward the sunset. He stared long into the dusk, as if to call up the Angel and yet another miracle. But this time, even though he stared and prayed for at least an hour, the Angel did not come and a miracle did not occur. He walked back to where Aaron stood waiting for him and said, "Let us walk a few more miles tonight. At least we'll be farther away from Shur than we are now. Maybe by then, something will happen and the walking will keep everyone's mind off their thirst."

"Sure," Aaron said, and slugged back through the sand to tell the parched Israelites that they were on the move again.

When the sun had long set and the dark night was slowing approaching the first rays of dawn, FrankieA, who was by this time quite dog tired but still ambling alongside Moses, crinkled his nose into the air and let out a short snort.

"Huummph," he barked.

"What is it, boy?" Moses asked. "Smell something?"

"Ruff-ruff-waaa-waaa," the hound responded, lowering his head so that his long ears could fold down and scrape up the faint scent into his nose.

Moses turned to Zipporah. "What's he saying now?"

"I think he's saying he smells water," she said.

Moses sniffed the air and then knelt to touch the ground. It was slightly damp, as if a soft rain had just fallen. "Well, I'll be. I suppose the little guy is right."

""Huummph," FrankieA barked. "Ruff-ruff-waaa-waaa."

"Hey, Aaron!" Moses called back to his brother, who was walking in the middle of the crowd with Joseph. "We found, that is, FrankieA found water!"

"Water! Water!" everyone began to shout to one another. "We found water!"

"Where?" Joseph asked.

"Here, there, everywhere! Water, water, everywhere," Aaron said, stamping the damp earth with his feet. "Look how squishy the ground is! There must be a lake or stream up ahead." And the Israelites pushed past him and Joseph pulling the carts with the empty water jugs behind them in their haste to quench their thirst.

When they reached the wide swamp whose waters where seeping into the ground, the people stopped and waded in, gleefully splashing each other with not only the water, but also with handfuls of mud and green, sodden reeds. When they began to drink the water, however, they quickly spat it out.

"Phew!" a little boy said. "What is this? It tastes like rotten bananas."

"No, no," said a little girl. "It's burnt eggs and molded lettuce."

"What is this place that you've led us to," her mother said to Moses, "to promise us water and then give us this dirty, foul liquid? It's not even fit for dogs!"

"Grrrr-ufffff-ruff!" FrankieA growled, as if to say, "I resent that!"

The others echoed her sentiment, complaining bitterly about the tainted water of the land and the empty promises of Moses.

"Hold on, woman," Moses said. "I am doing the best I can with what I got. I suppose there is a well somewhere above it that is spewing fresh water into the swamp. There must be something in the swamp itself that is causing the water to be tainted."

Joseph cupped his hands and scooped up a few sips of water. "Yeech!" he said after tasting it. "It is indeed bitter."

"Then let's call this place Marah, the Place of Bitterness," Moses said, "and move on." He began walking towards the east where the sun was, by this time, high in the sky.

Still complaining, the Israelites slogged out of the swamp and followed him.

FrankieA kept his nose to the ground, for he was quite thirsty, too, and would do anything for a few laps of fresh, spring water. A few strides ahead of Moses, he kept sniffing and walking, walking and sniffing, following his innate instincts when, quite late that very afternoon, tired of sniffing and walking without finding anything, he happened upon a stick of gopher wood small enough to carry in his mouth, yet big enough for Moses to toss. Now seemed like a good time to play fetch.

He carried the stick to Moses and dropped it at his feet.

"Not now, FrankieA," Moses said wearily. "I'm too tired. And too thirsty to think about playing with you now. Go find someone else." And with that, he picked up the gopher wood stick and flung it into the air, far ahead of the multitudes, towards the shallow foothills at the very edge of Marah.

"Arf-arf-rufff-hallloooooo!" the hound bayed, and then bounded after the tossed twig. It landed in a small, grassy knoll nestled amongst hillocks and craggy mounds. Seventy palm trees nearby bordered a small river and twelve springs bubbling up clear, clean, cool water.

"Arf-arf-rufff-hallloooooo!" he bayed again. He raced back and forth between the knoll between Moses and Aaron and Miriam and Zipporah and Joseph the Ammonite until they finally joined him under the palm trees.

"Arf-arf-rufff-arf-woof-woof!" he barked.

"Look," Zipporah said, pointing at the springs. "Look, Moses, your dog has found us water!"

And when they tasted the clean, unsullied liquid, they praised the Lord for giving the Basset Hound his wondrous sense of smell that found them this fresh water.

The people soon refilled their water jugs and repacked them on the carts with date palm fronds, made a meal of the palm fruit, and joining in hymns of praise, thanked God for their many blessings. They camped by the side of the river for the night in the oasis they called the Place of Elim because they were so elated. And there they stayed for a week and a day to eat and drink their fill.

Two months and fifteen days into their journey towards the Promised Land, the Israelites travelled through the Wilderness of Sihn and down into the Plains of Gazzieria. And while they had continued to praise God and Moses for providing for them, they also began to run out of food. There was nothing left of the unleavened bread they had brought with them except stale crumbs; nothing left of the dates and figs but gnarly pits and dried rinds. Soon, as their hunger increased, their tributes, adulations, and singing lessened. Finally, with empty stomachs and minds once again full of complaints about Moses and his inadequate leadership, they stopped and refused to go any further.

"What's this, now?" Moses asked of the Israelites, now sitting and lying on the ground clasping their stomachs and moaning about their emptiness.

"We've not eaten for days and have hunger pangs," Joseph said. "Aren't you hungry either?"

"Well, yes, I suppose," Moses replied. "But a little fasting can be healthy for you."

"Not for this long, my dear," Zipporah chided. "Look at the children. They are going to starve and grow gaunt if they don't have any nourishment soon."

"Well, they do look a little thinner," her husband agreed. "But what I am to do?"

"Find us food!" everyone yelled in unison. "Find us food! Find us food!" It became a chant that echoed across the land they were in, bouncing off the very Firmament of Heaven.

Left to his own devices, FrankieA the Basset Hound roamed and rambled through the multitude and out across the land way ahead of Moses and Aaron. He, too, was hungry and longed for a meaty bone to chew or a slab of unleavened bread to eat, slathered with the oily paste of nuts that Zipporah would often make for him back home. He hadn't eaten for days, and his ribs began to show through his once shiny black, tan, and white coat. His ears, normally droopy, drooped even more. But despite his hunger, he still hadn't lost his great sense of smell.

One morning, while out by himself in the wilderness, FrankieA was awakened by a loud sound of the flapping of many wings. He squinted into the sunrise and saw a host of quails sweeping and swooping across the sky, dipping in and out of the great, white cumulous clouds, forming a wide phalanx, occluding the sun itself. They cooed and cawed and cackled "kar-wit, kar-wit, ka-loi-kee, whoil-kee, whoil-kee, ka-loi-kee" as they flew.

Thinking of nothing else except that one might be a tasty morsel for breakfast, the Basset Hound began chasing them. He ran and ran under them as they flew higher and higher until his short, stumpy little legs couldn't carry him any farther. Finally, exhausted, he flopped down on the ground, alternately panting and gulping huge gasps of air. When he was almost breathing normally, he sat up and watched in wonder as the birds flew and circled overhead until, finally, they too, seemingly tired from all their sweeping and swooping, landed on the ground before him.

The birds and Basset stared at one another for a while, the Basset still panting, and the birds preening their wings and brown-speckled snowy white breasts. The sun continued to rise in the sky until it was exactly midway between both horizons. FrankieA yawned and stood up.

"Ruff," he said. "Time to find Moses. Maybe he has figured out a way to feed the masses."

And with that, the quails, startled by his words and actions, fluttered and flit and flew upwards again until they covered the early afternoon sky. Forming a huge "W", they took wing again towards the west. FrankieA shook his head at the sight, causing his long ears to swing back and forth, slapping against his jowls glistening with drool.

"Huh, hummrumph?" he chortled, gazing at the ground before him that the quail had taken off from. "What is this?" He tasted the white coating on the grass with his tongue and found it quite delicious, reminiscent of salami and aged cheese on sourdough bread.

"Yummm...arf...woof. Ahmannamannayum!" he exclaimed and went about eating as much of it as he could.

When he had eaten his fill and his belly was distended and he could no longer walk because he was so full, he again flopped upon the ground and slept. Towards evening, he was awakened once again by a gentle flapping of wings. There, haloed by the soft, orange luminescence of the setting sun hovered the Angel. Shards of quail feathers dotted his otherwise white wings.

"Was that you?" FrankieA asked—for, as you know, in the presence of Angels, animals can talk so that we humans can understand them. "You were the birds? You left all this food?"

The Angel nodded, then pointed to the salami, cheese, and sourdough feast that lay all around them, then pointed beyond, behind FrankieA to where Moses, Aaron, and the Israelites were camped.

"Oh, yeah, I almost forgot. I should tell them about this, huh?" the Basset Hound sniffed. "Okay, I will. Lead the way."

The Angel's head shook from side to side, meaning "No, you must do this yourself." And with a quivering of wings, the Angel floated higher into the sky and flew away.

FrankieA dragged himself up onto his massive, wide paws, turned to the west, and ambled back to Moses, Aaron, Miriam, Zipporah, Joseph the Ammonite, and the multitude of hungry travelers.

"Woof, woof, woof, woof, Yummm...arf...woof. Ahmannamannayum!" he barked when he finally roused Moses from his before-dinner nap. "Yummm...arf...woof. Ahmannamannayumyum!"

"What's that you're saying, FrankieA?" Moses grumbled, rubbing the sleep from his eyes. "Ahmannamannayumyum? What is that?"

"I think he is saying 'manna', my dear," Zipporah said, waking by his side. "Manna, you know…the bread of life, from Heaven. Your Basset Hound has found us food."

"I suppose," Moses said sleepily. But when he finally realized what his wife was saying, he bolted straight up out of bed and yelled, "Saints be praised! FrankieA has found us food!" He skipped out across the field, yelling, "Aaron! Aaron! Miriam! Joseph! Get up! Get up, everyone! Our Basset Hound has found us food!"

And so, for six days and six nights the Israelites feasted on the strange "manna" that tasted of salami and aged cheese on sourdough bread, washing it down with the cool, fresh water they had carted from the twelve streams in the Place of Elim. They never tired of the flavor, nor did they grumble or complain about being hungry or thirsty, ever again. In the evenings, Miriam played her tambourine, Zipporah thumped rhythms on her tambour, and everyone sang and danced and offered hymns of praise to God, who always seemed to provide for them through Moses, even if He did have the assistance of an Angel and FrankieA the Basset Hound.

Many months later, the Israelites were still wandering around in the deserts and wildernesses beyond Egypt across the Red Sea, still looking for the Promised Land. It, by now, seemed very elusive to them. Some despaired of ever really finding it. Others kept their faith in God and their trust in Moses. Still others, now inured to the life of nomads and wanderers, blithely trudged on wherever they were led.

One day, Moses looked up and found himself at the foot of Mount Sinai. During his childhood, while growing up as a beloved son in the household of Ramses II, the great Pharaoh of Egypt, he had heard of the mountain, its majestic peak rising high into the blue, azure sky—its slopes virtually unscalable and its summit impenetrable.

The Israelites were encamped in the fields and dales around the mountain, foraging for food and water at its base to supplement their supplies. In the years of travel, they had learned to make beer from the barley gleaned from farms they passed along the way, wine from grapes of arbors they walked through, and bread from the manna that God so graciously so often provided. And their fold, despite the earlier hardships, was beginning to prosper on this exodus from Egypt.

So much so, that they began to rail against the old laws of Yahweh that Moses and Aaron had insisted they keep during the long journey. It was getting harder and harder to keep peace and order in the multitude, especially with the younger adults, who thought there must be something better than wandering around in the desert, scavenging for food, water, and shelter, looking for what they were beginning to perceive as a non-existent Promised Land.

But Moses and FrankieA and, of course, Zipporah and Miriam and Aaron did not loose faith. They believed that just as He provided them with food and water, He would eventually lead them to the Promised Land. Joseph, however, wasn't all that sure. So, one day, he came to Moses standing at the foot of Mount Sinai and said:

"Go ahead, our fearless leader. Climb that mountain and see if you can't find God, if ever He truly does exist."

"Don't be silly, Joseph," Moses said. "Of course He exists. Didn't He deliver us from Pharaoh's army by parting the Red Sea and finding us food and water in the deserts and wildernesses when we ran out of our own supplies? And now, now we are at the foot of Mount Sinai, the greatest mountain in the world. Isn't it just grand? You've just got to believe!"

"All well and good, Moses," Joseph replied. "But we have still not found the Land as He, um, excuse the pun, promised."

"Yes, well, I suppose that will come in His own good time. But, for now, we need to concentrate, Joseph, on the blessings we have now... ample food and water and cozy shelter and good health and—many babies are due to be born to increase our fold..."

"But, if I may reiterate, Moses," Joseph retaliated, "we *still* haven't found the Promised Land. And, by my reckoning," he said, unfolding a huge handwritten map of the known world, "we are quite wide afield of it, having crossed and crisscrossed these many deserts and wildernesses many, many times over and over again. This is taking much longer than we expected, isn't it?" He waved the map at Moses, who stepped back and cowered.

"Yes, well, I suppose..." he said.

"You suppose, you suppose!" Joseph yelled. "You probably suppose your toes are roses, Moses. But you suppose erroneously!"

"But I, but I," Moses stammered. "I am doing the best I can with what I have. With what God gave me."

"Well, it's not enough!" Joseph exclaimed. He threw the map at Moses' feet and stomped off into the crowd of Israelites shouting mild invectives about the folly of their journey.

When Aaron and FrankieA heard the commotion Joseph the Ammonite was making, they came up to Moses to try and console him.

"He doesn't mean it. What he said means nothing," Aaron said, while the Basset Hound gently licked Moses' rosy toes peeking out from his sabots.

"I know that, but what he says mimics what the others are feeling," Moses said. "Right, Aaron? Am I right?"

"Well, yes," Aaron said, digging his own toes into the loamy dirt. "But it shouldn't matter. We are here at the base of this wondrous mountain for a reason."

"Yes, I suppose," said Moses. "But I wonder what it is."

He looked up at the mountain, and out of the corner of his eye, he saw a glint. Perhaps it was a reflection of the sun, or a streak of silvery-red ore, or perhaps the grey wing of an eagle catching the light. At any rate, Moses continued to chat with Aaron until they both heard loud barking and baying. They turned to the sounds and there, halfway up the southern slope of Mount Sinai, was FrankieA the Basset Hound, chugging along as best he could, climbing up to the summit.

"Hey, FrankieA!" Aaron shouted. "What do you think you're doing?"

"Silly dog!" yelled Moses. "Come down from there."

But the Basset Hound either didn't hear them or chose to ignore them, because he continued to climb up Mount Sinai.

"Obey me, you stubborn hound!" Moses roared. "Come back down here at once. Don't make me climb up there after you."

But FrankieA continued to climb, his stubby legs and massive paws clawing the slippery, craggy sides of the mountain for purchase.

"Looks like you may have to, Moses," said Aaron. "That hound of yours certainly has a one-track mind!"

"Oh, I suppose he does," Moses said, wrapping his cloak around himself to buffet the winds and planting his staff firmly into the ground before him. "Guess I'll have to go get him myself."

And Moses began to ascend Mount Sinai after FrankieA. Not sure where he was going, he used the silvery-red glint as a beacon and climbed up toward it, all the while calling for the Basset Hound to "Come! Come here, boy! Come on, FrankieA. Come to me!" But FrankieA did not come and, so, Moses climbed higher and higher toward the light until he ran out of mountainside and was standing on its very top, at the summit. The silvery-red glint had disappeared and so had FrankieA. But there, on the summit, in their place, was a large, grey-green and red bush that seemed to be burning with fire, yet was not consumed by the flames.

"What is this?" Moses asked in wonderment.

"Best to probably ask, 'Who is This'?"

Moses looked around, but couldn't see anyone. Where was the voice coming from?

"Where are you?" he queried, searching all around the summit.

"Here, right in front of you," the voice said.

"I see nothing but a burning bush," Moses sighed.

"Exactly," said the voice. "I am. I am the burning bush. At least for now."

"Don't be silly," Moses quipped. "Burning bushes cannot talk. Can they?"

"If they are God, then, yes, they can." The voice seemed to have a hint of a smile in it.

Moses stepped back, nearly toppling off the edge of the summit.

"Oh, my God," he said.

"Yes?"

"Well, I mean… I meant to say…"

"Yes, Moses. I know what you meant to say. But maybe now it's time that you listened."

Moses stood quietly while the bush slowly burned and shimmered as God composed Himself.

"Ahem," God began. "It seems on your long exodus from Egypt toward the Promised Land, the multitudes, my people, have been complaining and moaning about not having enough to eat and drink, even though I adequately provided food and water. Have I not?"

"Yes, well, I suppose you did."

"You suppose, Moses? Did I or did I not?"

"Yes, God, you did. Amply well…we were provided for. Yes, indeed."

"Thank you, Moses," God continued. "Now it's time the Israelites, before they enter the Promised Land, had a few laws, er, commandments.'

"Commandments?" Moses asked.

"Yes, commandments , instructions, if you will, to guide them along their way—and if they are kept in my honor and glory, then all will be right with the world."

And from the burning bush rose a large, spiking flame that carved out two large marble tablets, engraved with ten directives, into the side of the mountaintop.

God read them out loud as Moses knelt in awe and wonder. When He was finished, the flame carried the tablets to Moses and lay them at his feet.

"Will you promise me this, Moses?" God asked, "That these, my commandments, will be kept?"

"Well, yes, I suppo...No, I don't suppose. I promise!" Moses vowed.

And in that instant, FrankieA appeared from behind the bush and sat by Moses' side, looking up at him expectantly.

"Hallooooo-vooo-halloooo!" he howled.

"Say 'hello' yourself," said God from the bush. "You look vaguely familiar. Didn't I create you on the Eighth Day?"

"Ruffer," FrankieA said, and then bounded down Mount Sinai, followed by Moses carrying the tablets.

After the ten laws of God were presented to and accepted by the people that night, Moses and FrankieA sat with Aaron and Joseph under a cypress tree growing out from the side of the mountain.

"Did He really say we'd be entering the Promised Land soon, Moses?" Joseph asked.

"Yes, He did," Moses replied. "As I told you, you've just got to have a little faith." He smiled at his old friend, then turned to his brother. "Let's look at that map of yours, Aaron, and see exactly where we are."

Aaron took the large papyrus scroll from the folds of his tunic and unrolled it.

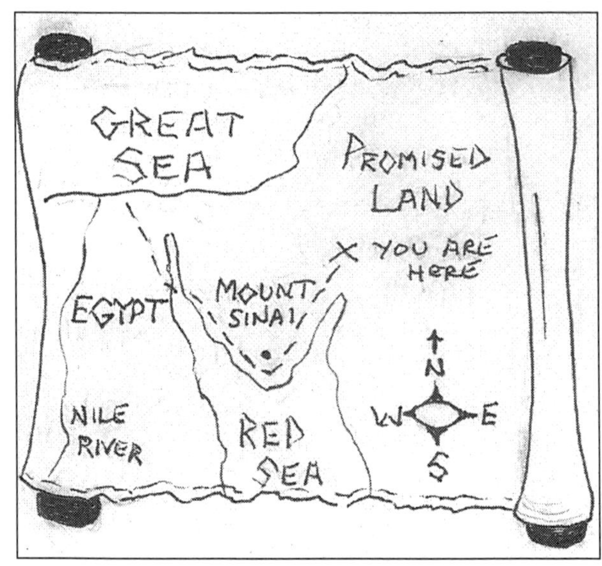

"We are here," he said, pointing to the black dot that represented Mount Sinai. "And to the best of my reckoning, the Promised Land should be here," he said, pointing far beyond the edge of the map. "Totally out of sight," he said, squatting on his haunches, "but I think that is the direction we should go."

"I suppose it is," Moses said. "We'll leave at first light."

The next morning just at the very beginning of dawn, Moses led the Israelites away from Mount Sinai travelling due north straight toward the land of Canaan where, as God had said, they were to settle. FrankieA joyfully trotted ahead of the crowd, with his white-tipped tail proudly wagging in the gentle desert breezes.

And so, while Moses supposed that they would reach the Promised Land in just a short while, the black, tan, and white Basset Hound was sure of it.

THE BLESSED BASSET OF BETHLEHEM

This ancient legend has been handed down through countless generations, literally from the first days of the time of Christ to today's times. It began as an oral tradition, told and retold in front of many an evening fire to inquiring adults and curious children. As a matter of fact, Joseph of Arimethea, who, legend tells us, brought the Holy Grail to the British Isles, first carried it to Ireland. Conveyed from father to son, mother to daughter by oral tradition, this story was first written down in the wooden strokes of Ogham in the mid-Fifth Century after Christ. It was later translated into the Gaelic in different Irish monasteries, the very same that saved civilization, during the Middle Ages. Because of the different translations, there are many different versions, especially of the ending. But of all of the original Irish tales, it maintains the basic, true original plot as I will shortly relate to you.

St. Francis of Assisi first heard the tale during his early travels as a crusader. When he left the life of merchant riches and feudal warfare, one of his first accomplishments as a hermit monk was to translate the story from old Irish Gaelic into coarsely written medieval Italian. St. Francis told and retold the tale to his followers, and often incorporated its basic themes into simple sermons, expounding its heroes in the verses of a number of his canticles. He, incidentally, changed his given name to the more saintly "Francis", in honor of this story's hero.

From the Franciscan monasteries of Italy, then, the story slowly migrated to Hubert of Ardennes, a mighty, bloodthirsty, and merciless killer of animals in the French forest. The hunter, when he heard the story, immediately stopped hunting and founded a monastery amongst the wooden glens he frequently hunted with his bow. Captivated by the loyal and unselfish nature of one of the first truly lowliest members of that first manger family, the monks, later to be known as the Monks of St. Hubert, recreated the breed from its then modern closest canine relative, the Bloodhound. The new strain of hounds grew, with the blessings and grace of God bestowed especially upon it that first Nativity, into the finest and most spiritual breed of hound we know today. That breed, of course, is the Basset Hound.

This, then, is the story of Frankie, the Blessed Basset of Bethlehem, a direct descendant of the very same Frankie who saved Noah's Ark from sinking, and of FrankieA, who helped Moses lead the Israelites out of Egypt to the Promised Land. In fact, this may be one of the greatest animal stories that have ever been told. This, in fact, is Frankie's tail, er, tale.

In those days there came a decree from Rome that all who lived in Palestine, in the country that we know today as Israel, the Holy Land, were to be counted as either citizens or slaves in this oppressed area of the Empire. That meant, according to the decree, that every male, animal as well as human, had to travel with his family to his town of origin; that is, to where his ancestors first began living, to register as residents of Palestine. The Governor reckoned that each family and its members could more easily be accounted for in its hometown. He did not think of the harsh difficulties such travels would incur upon his subjects. But, then, he never did consider them in any of his decisions.

And so it was, and just as well it was, that one morning, in the chilly month of Teth, a young family from Galilee -- but not the family that you might first think -- had to travel south from the village of Tulkarm to the City of Jerusalem. From Jerusalem, they traveled to its meager suburb of Bethlehem where they were to join a camel caravan heading northeast to Na'arm, their town of origin. The journey was to take many days to the City of David, and many more to their native town.

The family was of the house of Jabal. They were richer in money than they were in charity and compassion, and had no fellowship or peace with their brothers or neighbors. The traveling family consisted of a complaining mother, an obsequious father, two very spoiled children, many hungry goats, a barren cow, two swift horses, and three small, young, long-eared hounds. The hounds were named Frankie, Sensuous, and Myrrh.

And unlike the rest of the family, the hounds were the only kind, charitable members of this ragtag group now on its long, arduous journey.

Of the three hounds, Frankie was the youngest, the smallest, and the shortest. For unknown reasons, he was born without the long, lanky legs of his brother and sister. As he grew, his body lengthened, like theirs did; his ears widened, like theirs did; and his nose grew more powerful and sensitive, like theirs did. But his legs...well, his legs just didn't grow. They grew only so much, becoming short and stocky and stubby. Instead of being tall and lean, he was long and squat. Instead of running fast and sure and steady, he galloped in quick, clumsy bursts. And, because of his short, stocky legs, he took three times as many steps as his siblings did in order to travel the same distance.

Frankie was all of about a year old when his journey began. Uprooted from the muddy, flat backyard of his desert home, he was forced to walk for long, dreary days beside the motley caravan to Jerusalem. The road was dusty and rough, full of numerous potholes and millions of sharp rocks. At that time of year, in the middle of the Jewish month of Teth, the dark, gray winter clouds hung dankly overhead. The air was crispy cold, slicing through the thin folds of the family robes. It was a long, tiresome journey, especially for the dogs.

Although the father, bewailing the arduous journey that he had to take with family in tow to prove his loyalty to Augustus, the Caesar, provided generously for the human members of his family, he was not so very kind to the animals of his household. The goats were fed enough to keep them walking; the cow offered enough fodder to give just enough milk for the children's breakfast and the adult's afternoon tea; the horses just enough oats to give them energy to pull the olive wood cart for exactly eight hours. And the hounds? Well, the hounds were allowed to roam freely as they journeyed, fending and foraging and feuding amongst and for themselves for whatever morsels of food that they could find or catch in the desert sands.

Sensuous and Myrrh, the two oldest dogs, were silky sleek, and lithe, and tall of limb. They were able to quickly adapt to the harsh change in conditions from resting nightly by the warmth of their small stone cave on the outskirts of Tulkarm to sleeping among the sharp rocks along the side of the road. How easily they learned to fetch desert rabbit and to squander water squeezed from the juice of cactus. Frankie, on the other paw, er, hand, was the runt of the litter. The youngest, he was also the frailest with his very long body and amazingly short, stubby legs. His ears were so large and droopy, they dragged on the ground. Frankie constantly tripped over them with his huge paws as he tried to walk. He was so homely, in fact, that if you or I saw him today, we would say he was cute. Back then, however, not one member of his family, human or canine, wanted him. The goats totally ignored him; the cows only laughed. But they did let him tag along as best he could. The truth is, they simply didn't know quite yet what else to do with him except let him tag along as they ambled along the crowded road to Bethlehem.

Unlike the other hounds, Frankie was constantly being chided to keep up. "Quit lagging behind, ya lazy mutt! You're slowing us down!" the mother would cry. But Frankie was far from lazy. It was just that his legs were too short and he could barely run fast enough to catch up every time they slowed down. By the end of the day, while everyone else had energy to frolic and play, he was exhausted and would often cower under the wagon for rest, while one of his siblings, out of sympathy, brought him the meager dregs of oats for dinner.

"See how good-for-nothing he is?" The father admonished the children. "Why do you insist on keeping him when he does not even earn his own keep? He is nothing but a burden to us."

"Maybe in Bethlehem," the mother said, "we could foist him off on another family. Someone, not me, will see to his care and keeping. Certainly, as you say, he is unable to do so for himself." She then cackled, remembering the many times he had tried in vain to hunt with his brother and sister. Each time he started to chase a rabbit, Frankie doubled over, entwined in his own paws and ears, and falls in chagrin. For Frankie, you see, couldn't, rather, wouldn't, kill anything. He instantly felt a kindred spirit in each of the animals he chased. The sport became to him merely a game—not a method of providing food. As a result, he was teased by Sensuous and Myrrh; ridiculed by his human masters; and forced to eat the dregs of gruel and the daily leftover oats and fodder of the horse and cow and goats. Which, as you can surmise from the stingy nature of the humans, would not have been very much.

As they neared Bethlehem, the road became narrower and much more crowded. Many families of the house of David were converging on the small hamlet, with dusty dirt paths for streets and tilting lean-tos made of wood and stone. These were, literally, hovels for homes. Along the main street, across from the common fountain, stood the only solid structure in town. It was the Lowly Manger Inn. The inn's stout and hefty proprietors were among the many residents of Bethlehem, including, of course, the greedy Roman tax collectors, who were making a huge profit from the taking of the census.

However, the morning Frankie and his family arrived, the innkeepers had closed their doors to all who dared enter therein. Its rooms were full; its dining hall was overcrowded, and its stables were crammed with animals owned by the weary travelers.

"Go away! No rooms here," they lustily shouted from the slanting stone porch of their establishment.

"No room here. Go elsewhere. Anywhere. But not here."

And so it was upon hearing this that the family decided to meander through Bethlehem, beyond its borders, to the starlit fields in search of other shelter for the night. Frankie, of course, lagged far behind. He tried to keep up, barking for his brother and sister to wait, but they were too busy keeping track of the family wagon.

The crowd was much too noisy to hear his calls. Finally, in the crush and bustle of visitors to the tiny village, Frankie soon lost all sight of his family.

All he could see were the legs of strangers. All he could hear, above his own barking, were strange sounds. He couldn't understand the languages of many lands. He couldn't obey when foreign voices told him "Shoo!" and "Go away, mutt!" and "Go home!" If he could, he would have tried to tell them he wasn't a mutt. And he hadn't a home to which to go. But the strange legs kicked and the foreign voices frightened him. So, he sought the safety of a back alley, away from the maddening crowd.

And so, separated from his family, Frankie the Basset was thus forever lost in the swarming wilderness of downtown Bethlehem.

Or so you might think. For what Frankie lacked in size and might, he was more than compensated for in intelligence and resourcefulness. Not to mention his mighty powerful and sensitive sense of smell.

When he finally realized he was separated forever from Sensuous and Myrrh, he was greatly saddened. But then, he thought, they will have more to eat without me.

He was not so sad to have lost the company of the human family, however. Perhaps, in his large hound heart, he hoped there might be another family that would offer him not only a home, a warm hearth, but loving hearts. And so, that cold, dark, chilly evening, tossed and turned around by the insensitive tide of humanity into the icy streets of Bethlehem, Frankie began his search. His first goal was to find a bit of food and a warm place in which to curl up for the night.

But where would he find such a safe haven?

The streets of Bethlehem were crammed with travelers and tourists and many members of the house of David. Weary feet shuffled on the dusty ruts that served as streets, spewing up flakes of dry desert sands and village pollution: the dregs of dinner, the droppings of horses and camels; the effluvia of daily living in an old town much too crowded with residents even before the travelers arrived. Frankie's nose was soon clogged with so many smells, he quickly realized he could no longer separate the scents and, so, peering upwards from beneath the cloud of humanity, he saw a small clearing. A path wound its way off the main drag, along the alley alongside the Lowly Manger Inn, leading out of the crowds and into the empty countryside.

Pausing to lick his paws, sore from walking many miles, Frankie eyed the alley. He sneezed the dust out of his nose and snuffled. "There, there I must go," he howled.

With amazing speed for such short legs, he bounded through the throng and headed for the lane. He scampered between cart wheels, scurried behind camels, wending his way zigzagging across the rutted road in front of travelers and behind footed vendors hawking their wares to the weary. Finally, with many leaps and bounds, skirting betwixt and between the many feet that he thought were seeking to trample him down, he found himself alone in the middle of the small dirt path. It was small and narrow. From its dirt rut, the hound could hear the sounds of the travelers passing on the main street; the calls of street vendors plying their wares; the braying of laden donkeys and pack mules; the cries of distant parents calling their children to supper.

Now, as you might know, one of the miraculous qualities of Bassets, at least those today, is their great sense of smell. A hound's nose can pick up a million more pixels of odor than a human could ever imagine. And his ears? Why, do you really think they are for hearing? Call to a hound sometime while he is out in the field. He is won't be listening to you, but smelling many things. For the great length and shape of a Basset's ear flaps are not for picking up sounds, but for gathering scents along the ground, funneling them up into his great nasal cavities to sniff and snort and scout. You see, Frankie's greatest gift was his sense of smell. With one swift whiff, he could tell you all there is to know about any particular smell: where it came from, to whom it belonged, how old the person or animal was, where it came from, where it was going, and what it last ate and drank. His hound's nose was so powerful, he could smell, as the expression goes, a rat, or anything else for that matter, more than a mile away.

So, you might ask, and well you should, why didn't Frankie sniff up the trail of his family, if he was so lost and his sense of smell so good? Well, good question. And here is the good answer: A hound's sense of smell is second only to his good common sense. Answer me this: If you were once a member of a family that starved you and thought of you so little that they didn't even know you were lost, now wouldn't you, once lost, look for another family?

Aha! I thought so.

Besides, the atmosphere of Bethlehem that night was so clogged with so many different smells, they even confused Frankie. If he had wanted to, it would have been next to impossible to isolate the distinct scents of his former master and siblings from the thousands and thousands of odors that mingled in the cold air that night.

And so, lost to his family, but not to himself, Frankie decided that once he could separate out the many different smells, he would sniff out a new life. "Perhaps, perhaps," he thought, "there is a better way."

Stretching his back leg, and craning his neck to see up the dark recesses of the alley, Frankie noticed an open space with a field beyond.

"Surely," he sighed, heaving heavily to catch his breath, "surely, this could be the way."

The hound huffed a bit, and then began the journey up the alley towards the clearing outside of Bethlehem where the smells were not as many or mingled. Just a quarter mile or so beyond the back of the Lowly Manger Inn was a small cave. Hand-hewn to enlarge its size, it was cut into the side of one of the many small hills that dotted this area of the land. Frankie sniffed the alley as he padded his way away from the city.

Stopping to whiff a clump of clay, he picked up the smell of a faint wisp of perfume.

"This must be Jasmine, or essence of olive," he thought. It was faint, but suggestive enough to beckon him forward. He scooted to the left and sniffed a straggly bush. There, he inhaled the strong smell of wood shavings from carvings. Then he scooted to the right and sniffed some more.

"Why, a carpenter has passed by here no more than a few hours ago," he surmised.

A few more sniffs to the right, and he picked up the sweat of a tired donkey. Frankie stopped short at the merest whiff of. . .

"What is this?" he whimpered to himself. He couldn't quite tell; but it permeated his body and caused his heart to tremble in delight.

The smells were warm and kind and loving. Most of all, they were inviting; as if to say, "Come be part of us. You will be loved."

Frankie sat very still and cocked his long muzzle to one side, as if recognizing a familiar sound or sight in the near distance. He sniffed the air once more, just to make sure.

And then:

"These, these!" he suddenly howled in glee. "These are the scents of my new family."

Hesitating no longer, Frankie bounded up the remaining length of the alley and careened his little, long, stubby short-legged, body onto the rolling pasture and ran pell-mell towards the cave. He slid head first onto the marshy-iced grasses and, because he wasn't watching where he was going, caromed into the leather thronged and woolen-wrapped legs of a tall shepherd.

"What have we here!" the shepherd exclaimed, roughly picking Frankie off the ground by the folds of the nape of his neck. He peered into the hound's solemn and sadly sagging, deep brown eyes.

Frankie could only manage a choked "arf".

"Ah, a vocal lad, we have, is it now? And what might ye be after here, my little, short-legged friend?"

Frankie choked off another "arf", to convey he was after following the carpenter and his family who smelled of Jasmine and donkey and home.

"Talking a'back to me, now, are ya?" the shepherd yelled, shaking the little hound so hard he yelped to be free.

"And sassing me back, don't ya know? So tell me, one of wee little legs, from whence do you come and to where are ye be going?"

Frankie, gasping for air, didn't, couldn't answer. He vainly pawed the empty space between him and the shepherd's face, struggling to be put down.

"Ack, you're a feisty one. I canna hold you no longer. Here, ya mangy pup, be on your way." With a sharp shake and a friendly kick, the shepherd put Frankie back onto the grass and nudged him with his sheep-skinned toe.

"Arf, arf, woof, arf, arf, woof, wooof, woof, woof," Frankie offered by way of gratitude for being let down. "Thank you. Thank you, kind sire. There's a family in that yonder cave and I think it's just had a baby," he said.

"What's that?" the shepherd queried, bending down to pet Frankie's long, silken coat, amazed that the little canine could talk. "You've got a message for us, lad?"

"No, not really," Frankie barked, for he miraculously realized that the human understood what he was saying, in his own canine language. It was, in fact, truly a night of miracles, as I am sure you know. "I just wanted to say that there's a family I wish to adopt, having lost my own along the way to Bethlehem, and they smell just grand."

"And where might they be?" the shepherd asked, calling his fellow sheep keepers in from the field to meet this amazing hound.

"There, yonder, in the cave carved out of the side of that hill," Frankie replied.

"Why, it looks to me like the stable of the Lowly Manger Inn," another shepherd quipped. "Heard tell there's neither room in their own barn nor rooms this night."

"Look," another pointed out, "there's a light in the cave."

And upon his spoken word, the heavens opened and a wide shaft of brilliant light cascaded across the horizon.

"Ach!" he exclaimed. "What is that?"

For lo, a host of angels appeared floating in the light, illuminating the skies.

They settled over the top of the cave and began to sing. "Be ye not afraid, shepherds, for we bring you tidings of great joy. For unto you and all nations is born this night a Savior who will be know to you as Jesus and will bring Peace and Light into the world. "

"Wow," the first shepherd said. "Is it finally the time for our savior, the Messiah to be born? Is he here, among us now?"

And one angel of the Lord said, "Yes, truly I say unto you, this night, your savior is born, in that cave yonder."

Extending a long, silken arm, the angel pointed the way. "Go," it sang, "go and see your Messiah."

"Ah, I dinna know," the second shepherd said. "This is pretty scary stuff. I dinna think the Lord to come in our lifetime. What will we do?"

Frankie nuzzled the bare, gnarled hand. He woofed, "Be not afraid, for unto us a child is born and unto us a child is given and his name shall be Emmanuel." He pressed the hand forward.

"Come on, let's go," he urged the shepherd. "If nothing else, at least, to see the baby."

With great trepidation, in the hopes of finding his true family, Frankie led the rag tag host of shepherds across the meadow to the cave. There, amidst the straw and bedding of animals, between the sheltering gaze of the carpenter who smelled of wood shavings and the young woman with the faint scent of Jasmine, the harried hound saw a small, beautiful child lying in the manger.

"Why, he's wondrous," one shepherd exclaimed.

"He's migh-ti-ous," another expounded.

"Glorious," the third exhaled.

"He's cold!" woofed Frankie. From his stance in front of the manger, the hound could easily see that the soon-to-be Savior of our known world was freezing in his thin swaddling clothes. The new Lord shivered so much in his manger that it almost shook the ground beneath the cave.

"Ah, excuse me?" the first shepherd said. "Who are you to criticize our Lord?"

"Well, the fact is, he is cold," barked Frankie back. "Look at him, shaking that rickety wooden manger to its very foundations with his frigidity. Those swaddling clothes, well meaning though they be, just ain't enough for this cold Bethlehem night."

"So, fledgling pup," the second shepherd snorted, "what do you intend to do? Build a fire by rubbing two paws together?"

"No, I intend on warming him up with my own body heat!"

And with that, without as much as by your leave, the little long Basset hound joyfully, but ever so carefully, approached the side of the manger. He barked softly to the babe's mother, as if to ask permission. She glanced kindly at the carpenter who smiled. Then, when the gentle nod from Mary was given, Frankie placed his front paws onto the side of the manger and allowed himself to be hoisted into the makeshift cradle.

There was just enough room for Frankie and the babe, but the hound managed to nuzzle some straw into a pile alongside the newborn. He then, oh so very gently and so very carefully, lay down on his side and stretched his long back upon it, daring to rest his head on the very same hay-filled pillow upon which the Savior was resting his head.

"Well, willya look at dat," the first shepherd exclaimed, as he moved out of sight of the second and third of his comrades. "Just as if he belonged there, the wee, little fellow."

And no sooner had he hopped in with, and settled against him, when the swaddled, mangered babe began to stop shivering. It didn't take long for the baby to warm up to the kind hound.

Now, the legend continues, Frankie slept with our Savior for at least eight days, until the three wisest men from the East came. They sought the new king who, the Hebrew prophets predicted, would be born in Bethlehem. For almost a year, they followed a double star shining in the East beyond them far to the small manger in the rough-hewn cave of the Lowly Manger Inn. Bowing reverently to view the babe, the three men were amazed to find him being quietly cuddled by a hound with short legs and massive ears.

"What manner of dog is this?" Gaspar, the youngest Magi, asked.

"He is, I am told by the Shepherd who understood his arfs and woofs, a Basset of the Frankie, Sensuous, and Myrrh family," Mary replied.

"Then we give our gifts in honor of his breed," Melchor smiled. "For so great is the heart of this, the smallest of its members, that he truly gave of himself to keep your son warm on the coldest nights of this year."

Years later, it was written that the three men, themselves kings, gave the Baby Jesus their offerings of Gold, Frankincense, and Myrrh, in tribute to the Basset who warmed Jesus the first few weeks of His life among us.

Shortly after the Three Kings departed, the shepherds returned to the fields to keep their flocks by night. Hearing a rumor nasty King Herod of Israel wanted to kill their son, Mary and Joseph fled south. The legend states thet Frankie, who because of his short stature made every one laugh, but mostly because of his large and gentle heart and demeanor, went with them. Once Frankie found where he truly belonged, he became the blessed childhood mascot of Jesus, sitting by his side as the boy learned Hebrew and studied the ancient Scriptures. While in Egypt, he became the grand sire of the Egyptian Basenji hounds, the forerunners of our modern-day bloodhound. And, as you know, it was from the bloodhound that the monks of St. Hubert recreated today's Basset.

When the family finally returned to Nazareth, the hound served for a while in Joseph's woodworking shop as guard and companion. Beyond that, nothing else is known.

But others claim that because of Frankie and his gift of warmth to the Baby Jesus, all earthly animals are today blessed with human speech each Christmas Eve.

And, more especially, because of Frankie, each and every Basset hound is the loyalest, most loving, most sincere, and the truest pet any human could have.

Now, anyone who has ever had one as a companion certainly knows this to be the gospel truth.

Amen.

PART II:

MODERN TIMES

FRANKIE: AN EVENING'S WALK

When we first met, he was no bigger than the length of my forearm, a tad too skinny for a Basset Hound puppy, napping nestled between his litter mates in the back of the Plexiglas pet store cage. I suspected he was the runt, smaller than the others; however, he was the feistiest. And, I surmised, perhaps the brightest. No sooner had I walked up the aisle, he was awake and bounding his way to the front of the cage. He clawed and scrabbled at the glass, pawing to get out, pawing to get my attention.

He started to chortle, a low whining from deep in his puppy throat. If I didn't know any better, I would think he was trying to talk—the rudiments of speech, analogous to a human baby's first words. But, I did think, that was not possible. Basset Hounds don't really *talk*. Or do they?

I was not shopping for or even planning on "adopting" a Basset, or any other kind of dog for that matter. I had merely stopped in the local pet store to buy two cases of cat food for my feline family while on my way to visit a friend who had just rented a carriage house in the country. But, he was so cute and persistent and had captured my full attention. What harm would it do to at least pet the little fellow? So, I put down the cat food cases in the aisle, sat on them, and asked the pet store attendant if I could please meet the puppy.

No sooner was he placed into my arms when he snuggled into my neck and promptly peed down the front of my new pale green, silk blouse. I was at first agitated, but then was quickly bemused to see what might have been first a look of chagrin and then a bemused smile of his own crossing his jowls and lighting up his hazel-brown eyes. I had no recourse but to smile wanly. He had, obviously, marked me as his own for life.

'What's your name, little fella?" I asked into a velveteen ear,

He muffled a plaintive "Woofie, woof", which I instinctively heard as "Frankie".

And so, as you rightly surmise, instead of continuing with my afternoon visiting plans, I brought him home.

It was the start of his very long life as my faithful and vociferous companion.

I remember when growing up my father often teased my mother about having a "long, short dog, with big droopy ears" around the house. He was enamored with Cleo, the Basset Hound, who starred in the popular TV show, "The People's Choice". Cleo had quite pithy and witty comments about her human family's lives, which amused Dad—my father was a very punny guy. Or maybe it was her long, sleek, pudgy body that attracted him, but forever after, Bassets were his favorite breed. He constantly pestered Mom, like a little kid, and teased me about having a pet, egging me on to pester her, too for a chunky, low-slung hound with the hang-dog face. But she was quite adamant in her refusals.

We could never really figure out why, except that once she did hint at having a canary that flew away when she, on a whim, opened the cage door while she was cleaning it on the patio. That loss, brought about by a brief lapse of attention, must have been very devastating. Apparently, she was quite attached to the bird and its escape to apparent freedom closed her heart to being attached to any animals again.

Had not Mom opened the cage door and the bird flown away, who knows how our lives might have been different? Perhaps had not her heart been hardened to loss, we would have had in my childhood a second Cleo or a first "Frankie".

"No pets in the house!" she dictated to my father. To me she said, "When you grow up and have a home of your own, you can have all the pets you want."

And that's exactly what I did.

It is in those nexus moments that we experience and so vividly remember when a quick, brief decision is made that changes our lives forever. And so it was with the tri-colored puppy nestled in my arms as I sat upon two cases of cat chow in the middle of a pet store isle. Since then I've often wondered what both our lives would have been like had I not made the decision to make him the focal point of my animal family.

Frankie was my third dog, but my first real canine pet.

His first predecessor was a Cocker Spaniel that I bought—actually, "borrowed" from some friends in Akron, Ohio who raised the breed as show dogs. The plan was for me to raise her from puppyhood to her first or second year, when we'd travel around the country showing her. Her pedigree, I learned, was quite "pure"—a string of champion show winners were her ancestors and this blonde beauty was sure to take all the blue ribbons she strove for. Despite her lineage and "best-in-show promise", however—you'd think with that background and potential, she'd be a bit better behaved--she was very high strung. The nervous, yappy type, you know? She barked loudly and shrilly at just about everything and everyone that walked by my first-floor duplex apartment. At night, she whined in her crate and if I cradled her in my arms in bed, she'd pee on the linens and howl in my ear. No amount of training or attention from me, let alone two obedience classes and private training, would stifle her edginess and voraciousness, nor prevent her from chewing up my favorite pair of Bass Weejun loafers or from swiping and eating defrosting ground sirloin off the kitchen counter.

To say the least, we did not get along. So, with great reluctance, I gave her back to the breeders, convinced that I really wasn't cut out to raise a puppy even as a pet, let alone one slated to make a life in the dog show world.

Frankie's second predecessor was a stray, motley-colored miniature Sheltie. I acquired her or, rather, she acquired me, when, on an evening's walk through the park, I saw her being beaten with the end of her leash by her then current owner for not walking properly beside him. She seemed to be a few years old, but still young enough to require a bit of training. She was crouching away from him, whining and straining at the leash to escape, as he mercilessly pounded her nose, shoulders, and rump.

"Hey, you!" I yelled at him. "Stop beating her. No one deserves that kind of treatment, not even a dog!"

Without hesitation, as if looking for an excuse, he offered the leash to me and said, "Okay, of you can do any better, then you take her!"

And that's how I acquired "Nestlee", whom I named for her dark chocolate eyes (also because I couldn't envision myself calling for a dog named "Hershey".

Nestlee loved to go camping—I was employed by a mid-western Girl Scout Council at the time—and would on command flush birds out of the reeds by the streams that we walked along. Someone had taught her to circle "left!" or "right!" on both verbal and visual cues, and it was a joy to watch her run and herd rabbits and, on occasion, other dogs in the field. She was also adept at corralling the younger Brownies. She was a big hit with the scout mothers, as Nestlee doubled as a sitter for their young children during troop meetings for the older girls and staff meetings.

I remember many autumn afternoons together, walking in the woods behind our apartment complex, and sitting on the patio in the early evenings after dinner watching the sunset behind the far distant Blue Ridge Mountains. Nestlee wasn't so much a talker as a listener and when we sat together, her head resting placidly upon my knee, she'd patiently hear my many stories of life growing up and my plans for our future. She was a joyous and companionable friend, always eager to please, never leaving my side except, of course, to herd—but only on command.

Sadly, however, after three years of companionship, I had to give up "Nestlee" when, for a multitude of reasons, I had to move back east and couldn't take her with me. She must have been five or six at the time. It was a sad day when I begrudgingly dropped her off at the shelter and saw her forlornly and dejectedly watch me walk away as I left her leaning listlessly at the cage bars. My only hope was (it still is) that someone did adopt her and that she joyously found a good home to pass her remaining years.

One can only hope. It's the only way I can still, to this day, assuage my guilt. And to promise, the memory of her eyes boring into my back as I sauntered away, that I would never leave another animal that way again; which is probably why I make it a point to contribute to the local private animal shelters in the area whenever I can.

It wasn't until Frankie came along at least fifteen years later that I allowed myself the luxury of owning a dog again—or, rather, having a dog who owns me.

For that was exactly the nature of our relationship. I was completely and utterly Frankie's human. When I brought him to our first home together, a rented house on the edge of a state park, he totally took over. It soon became evident that I was the one honored to live in his house, not he in mine. I also had the pleasure of driving his little red sports car, not the Toyota Supra that was, at the time, *my* dream machine. When he quickly grew bigger—into the forty-five plus pounds of compact muscle and loose, foldable skin—than the coupe's front passenger seat, for his safety I had to trade it in for a green Jeep Cherokee with a large cargo area in which he, the cherished hound, could comfortably ride. The choice was either him or the car and we know the only obvious choice, of course, was the hound. Any true dog lover would, without hesitation, have done the same.

Frankie turned out to be indeed cute and loveable. He grew into an intelligent and humorous cohort, just as the American Kennel Club Breed standard promised, fulfilling all of the traits, behavior, qualities, and persona characteristics of a typical Basset Hound, despite his nefarious background. I had soon learned that being sold by a pet store, he was probably a puppy mill puppy, with all the eventual health problems inherent with that kind of background. However, at this time in our life together, the most obvious trait was his ability, believe it or not, to talk.

When Frankie first came into my life, or, rather, mine into his, I was recovering from a major illness and renting a small farmhouse, the back yard of which abutted a state park. In the first year or so together, on cool summer and fall mornings, he loved to bound out the back door and race through the thickets, chasing birds and rabbits. It was therapeutic for me to watch him frolic and gambol in the woods, the early rays of the sun glinting off his sleek, shiny black, white, and tan coat. I would walk slowly behind him, carrying his leather leash, occasionally throwing sticks for him to catch.

When he was just a few days home, knowing that Bassets like to wander, following the scents that they pick up with their incredibly sharp sense of smell, I began smearing a glob or two of peanut butter on the backs of my sneakers, which Frankie eagerly nipped at as I walked. Thus, I had trained him from the very beginning to stay with me. And so, during our morning jaunts, with him bounding off-lead, he did not stray very far, always running back to me from time to time for another whiff of my shoes, a vigorous scratch behind his ears, and, perhaps, a liver treat from the plastic sandwich bag I concealed in the pocket of my jeans.

One morning, however, as we were in the back yard, practicing "sit" and "stay" for a basic puppy obedience class we were taking, a fawn stepped out from the bushes that separated our yard from the park forest. It didn't take much for her to be startled by Frankie's insistent barking at her. As she turned tail and ran away, he broke from me and raced after her. I heard his yapping and howling grow fainter and fainter as he gave chase away from me farther and farther into the woods. I tried following after him, calling his name and ordering him to "Come!"—an obedience command we hadn't quite yet mastered. No amount of smeared peanut butter, I knew, would lure him back.

I searched the woods and surrounding parkland for hours, calling and calling, but found neither hide nor tail of either Frankie or the fawn. The more I searched without finding him, the more my sinking feeling grew that my precious puppy would be lost forever. Finally, after spending the morning and the better part of the early afternoon wandering around in the park woods in what was a fruitless search, I decided to head back to the house for a late lunch, and to call the local humane society and police to report a missing dog. Dejected and sad, I walked slowly up the path out of the woods to our backyard and across the lawn to our back door.

I was uncertain, at first, what the black and white lump on the doorstop was, not trusting my eyesight or my raising hopes. But, there, on the stoop, much to my delight and surprise, was Frankie curled up into a neat bundle on the Welcome mat, taking a nap!

Needless to say, while I was flabbergasted to see him, he did not seem at all surprised to see me, as if sleeping on the stoop after a long romp in the woods with a fawn was the most natural thing in the world for him to do. He yawned when I petted him, and deigned to be jubilantly smothered in hugs and kisses with long caresses behind his ears.

From then on, I never doubted that whenever he did venture off, he would always return home to me.

As Frankie grew, he exhibited the common Basset trait of being sociable, both with humans—young as well as old—and with other animals. He got along famously with my two cats and enjoyed batting their plush toys around the kitchen floor, much to their annoyance. It wasn't long before he and Sammy, the Coon Cat were best buddies. Wally, on the other hand, was a much older cat and remained aloof to the morning play in the kitchen as I fixed breakfast or to the almost constant mewlings and chortlings between feline and canine as Frankie and Sammy called to one another throughout the house.

As I said, I could swear Frankie was learning to talk.

One early autumn evening, just a few days after moving from the farmhouse at the edge of the park to a newly purchased townhome in a development that also bordered a small, suburban wooded area, along French Creek, I settled on the plush damask-covered couch in the small living room still crammed with unopened boxes and stacks of unpacked, but still unshelved, books and records. My thought was to take a respite from unpacking and start reading a new historical novel that I had picked up while grocery shopping that morning, and to spend the rest of the day totally immersed in the last ten years of the 19th century.

Well, anyway, that was my thought. But, apparently, it was not Frankie's. For no sooner had I nestled into a plump array of plush cushions and read the first few pages of chapter one of the John Jakes paperback, when he leapt upon my lap and poked his nose into my face.

"I want a walk," he yelped.

"What?"

"A walk. I want a walk!"

"But, Frankie," I said, from the reverie of reading, still not realizing I was conversing in English with my Basset Hound, "you've just been out to do your, um, 'stuff'. Do you have to go out again?"

"Explore the woods..," he grumbled. "Lots of smells!"

"You want to explore the woods beyond the path behind our house?"

"ARF!"

"Tonight?"

"ARF! ARF!" And then he began his slow, soft, keening whine that I just could not resist. And so, I begrudgingly closed the book, got up, and grabbing his lead and a lightweight jacket from the newly installed row of pegs in the hallway to the kitchen, accompanied him out the back sliding door, down the deck stairs, onto the path that led from our tiny backyard into the woods.

Unlike the unruly forest of the park where we last lived, the suburban woods were rather pristine. There were a series of convoluted paths paved with wood shavings and tiny pebbles that wound in and around the trees, crisscrossing each other as they interwove through the woods. Soft pink and orangey-yellow rays of the last of the afternoon sun sparkled through the leaves of the uppermost branches, which looked like they had been trimmed to prevent overgrowth and crowding. Birds, hidden in them, twittered and a few squirrels, finishing the last of their day's foraging, chittered as they skittered across newly fallen leaves and wild grasses.

Frankie cocked his head at each twit and chit, listening. It was almost as if he understood what the birds and squirrels were saying. Well, I thought to myself, if he could speak English to humans, I am sure he could speak animal languages as well. And could probably translate, too; but I didn't ask.

Frankie, off lead, bounced along in front of me, running a few paces ahead, stopping and turning to see if I was following him, then bounding away ahead of me again. We continued along the main path until it curved behind a stand of oaks, revealing a portion of the bank of the creek—a small, sandy beach divided by a fallen tree trunk. It edged a wide and deep section of the creek.

Frankie bolted and ran onto the beach, mounting the log with his front paws, barking and howling loudly at the water.

"Ruff! Whooowl-ooowl! Swan!"

"What?" I asked breathlessly, running to catch up with him. "What did you say?"

"Look," Frankie indicated by turning his head and wagging his tail. "A swan."

And there it was, gliding majestically across the creek towards us, its head gracefully bobbing on his long, S-shaped downy-white neck. Now, I am not that much of a bird watcher, but I do know a bit about swans and identified this one as a male Mute Swan. Normally an inhabitant of regions farther north, it seemed a little strange to see one sailing around a creek in eastern Pennsylvania. And a bit odder to see a small sailor cap daintily perched upon his head, with two red and white ribbons streaming down the swan's neck

Frankie was stock still, his paws firmly planted on the log. As the cob[1] glided closer, he started a low, soft growl. The swan responded with a grunt and then a hoarse whistle. They definitely seemed to be communicating.

"Who are you?" Frankie barked.

"I am Cygnus Olor," the swan grunted with great dignity, as if one could emit a dignified grunt. This is what Frankie translated to me—all I heard from the swan were grunts and whining whistles. "But you can call me Cid."

"Where are you from, Cid?" my hound howled.

"The Great Lakes, originally. Erie."

"Are they that weird?" I chimed in when Frankie howled back to me what Cid told him. But either Frankie

---

[1] A male swan. Females are called pens.

didn't hear me in his excitement of talking with the swan or he chose not to translate the pun.

"Where are you going?" Frankie howled again.

"Well, I was on my way to join my bevy[2]. We plan on wintering along the inner banks of the Chesapeake, but I was detained at home. I am the arbitrator for the family of waterfowl known as Anatidae[3] and I had to settle a territorial dispute between the ducks and geese. It took longer than I thought, and I left the colony later than the rest of my fellow swans.

"It was already snowing in western New York and I got lost in a storm..." He looked around at his surroundings. "After much tumbling about in the fierce air currents, I was blown way off my course. So, too exhausted to fly on, I landed here. Nothing here looks familiar. Where am I?" he whistled.

Frankie looked at me quizzically.

"Tell him 'French Creek', in a small town a few miles outside of Philadelphia," I offered. "And ask him what he has on his head."

---

[2] The proper name for a flock of swans, consisting of ten to 100 members.
[3] The name for the family of waterfowl consisting of swans, geese, and ducks.

Cid looked haughtily down his black and orange beak at me as if I had just asked him why birds had wings. It was, as he finally deigned to explain that it was the most natural thing in the world for a swan to be wearing a sailor's hat, especially a French Canadian cob.

"And if you know my native tongue's word for 'hat', it is," he snorted, then hissed at me, "quite an 'a pros-chapeau'!" That said, he glided indignantly away from the small beach. He began to swim in circles, occasionally dipping his head and long neck into the water—with his white, tufted tail sticking straight up into the air. Each time he dipped, he came up with a strand of marsh grass which he casually ate while eyeing us wearily as my dog and I sat on the log watching him eat.

"Phil-a-del-phi-a," Cid grunted, after slowly chewing and swallowing his fourth strand of grass. "Is that near Maryland?"

"Not quite. You're a little off your mark," I said. "You need to go about another 100 miles or further south—as, if you'll pardon the saying, the crow flies."

"And how far is it if a *swan* flies?" Cid mused. "We do have a much large wing-span, you know." As he said this, he raised his upper body half way up out of the water, spreading his wings out to their full eight-foot span. He fluttered and flapped them while busking[4], churning up the muddy waters of French Creek until they were frothy, white foam.

I waited until the swan and the waters settled down.

"Same distance, depending upon weather conditions and wind speed," I explained with Frankie as my interpreter.

"Huh," Cid honked. "And how do I get there?"

"You fly, you silly goose," Frankie barked. At this, Cid bristled again, until the hound realized his mistake. "I take that back. You silly swan!"

"Can you follow simple directions?" I called across the waters. "If I drew you a map, could you read it?"

"Of course," said Cid. "I do believe I am a fairly accomplished, if not the largest, and the oldest species of the Anatidae family. I can read."

---

[4] Busking is when a male swan rises out of the water with his wings half raised. This is typically done when agitated or when a cob wishes to pose a threat.

"Indubitably," Frankie howled. Was that a smirk I saw on his face? Or was that just my overwrought imagination? An educated swan, indeed.

I fumbled in my jacket pocket and found my small writer's notebook and my ever-faithful Waterman pen (I never leave home without it), and, opening the pad to a blank page, began drawing a simple map that Cid could follow. As I sketched, Frankie and Cid once again engaged in conversation; the swan swimming in lazy circles in the middle of the creek; the hound sitting close to the water's edge. Gentle waves created by the swan gently lapped at his front paws.

"What's it like to be able to float like that upon the water?" Frankie asked Cid.

"Divine. Simply divine. Can't you swim, dog? I thought all members of your species could swim."

"Not I. I'm a Basset Hound. My bones are too heavy, and my legs are two short to carry me afloat."

"A pity," said the swan. "You don't know what you're missing. Or what you can do if you just tried." Cid paused. "Say, what's it like to be able to bound freely through the woods?"

"You mean run?"

"Yes. What is that like?"

"I suppose, when I am off lead and allowed to, it is like flying!"

"Oh, nothing is as great as flying, my furry friend. Nothing," said Cid, busking again. "To swoop and soar and flap one's wings, coasting on the edge of the wind..."

"How do you do that?" Frankie growled, sitting up on his hind legs and pawing his forelegs into the air in a vain—or is that 'vein'?---attempt to imitate the swan.

"Oh, it's just a habit of mine," Cid said, "like you scratching your ear with your hind leg or you, um, licking below your belly. Just the nature of the beast."

"Hey, guys, I hate to interrupt," I said, finishing Cid's map and holding it out to him. "Here is your map. It's relatively easy. Once you're in the air, head west, straight toward the setting sun, then turn left when you see the six lane highway just before the city. Follow that for two hours. Watch for the signs to Baltimore. Can't miss it."

"Okay, got it. Thanks," said Cid, snatching the folded map with his small-toothed beak and concealing it in the folds of his left wing. "I think I can follow that."

And with a great whoosh of his wings, he busked once more and lifted himself from the creek waters, rising majestically into the air. The vibrant throbbing of his wings in flight filled the night around us like faint, distant thunder announcing an approaching storm. I could only imagine what a bevy of flying geese would sound like—an on-coming freight train rumbling down steel rails.

"Thank you, my friends!" he trumpeted, and then, soaring up over the trees, disappeared into the sunset, leaving Frankie and me breathless on the beach. After all, we did converse with a swan and helped it find its way. How awesome is that?

Frankie and I continued our walk, hoping to reach the end of the main path and be half way back again toward our house before the sun had fully set. But walking a Basset Hound is, at best, a series of short strolls interrupted by frequent stops to sniff and "water the ground". Frankie was a quick ambler when he got up a head of steam and had a direction in mind. Yet, more often than not, he had to stop to sniff just about every blade of grass or fallen leaf, often peeing on it, which easily stretched a normally ten or fifteen minute walk into one lasting forty-five minutes.

During one pit stop, not far from where we met Cid, I heard footsteps crunching the wood chips and pebbles behind us. A little leery of meeting strangers while walking my dog in the evening, I tried to hasten Frankie along. But when a child's shout, "Huckle-ber-ry! Blue-ber-ry!" pierced the air, there was no diverting him from the new sounds.

Frankie turned away from sniffing and raced back past me to the young girl and the adult who seemed to be searching the woods. My hound was excited to see them, and could not contain himself as he barked, howled, and twirled in front of them, begging for attention. Since our move, we were so busy unpacking and arranging our new home, we really had not ventured out to meet anyone, except for one or two neighbors at the mailbox kiosk or hauling a bag of recyclables to the dumpster. Frankie, it seemed, was starved for other company besides mine.

"Arf, Woof woofie—Hello, my name is Frankie," he said. Of course, the other humans only heard "Art. Woof woofie". I heard the "Hello, my name is Frankie" part. As they drew closer, with Frankie literally bouncing around them, I recognized the gentleman. He and his family—wife and daughter—lived two doors down from me in the end unit with a large, wrap-around deck. I had met him at the dumpster a few evenings ago while throwing out a stack of flattened cardboard packing boxes.

"Hi, Dan," I said in greeting.

"Hi!" He bent over Frankie and vigorously rubbed his shoulders. "This must be Frankie. My word, why is he so excited?"

"He's glad to see humans other than myself," I explained. "This must be your daughter."

"I'm Mary," she said, wiping a small tear from her eye.

"Hi Mary. What's wrong?"

"We lost our pets, Huckleberry Rabbit and Blueberry Bunny,"

"Someone forgot to close the latch on their cage on our porch, and they got out," Dan said. "We didn't notice until after dinner when Mary here went to feed them. We followed their tracks on the mud to this path and then lost their trail."

"Now we'll never find them," Mary sobbed.

"It's okay, sweetheart," Dan tried to comfort his daughter. "I am sure they're around here somewhere."

"Howl, hooo, howhooo. Arf, woof-woof-woof! Arf, woof-woof-woof!—I can find them, I can find them!" Frankie said.

"I'm sorry to hear that. Maybe my hound, Frankie, can help you," I offered.

"That is a great offer, but you don't think he'd scare them farther away?"

"Rabbits, Dan, are his specialty," I said, clipping Frankie's lead onto his collar. "Come on, boy, time to go to work."

Two sessions of our second year obedience class were devoted to scent tracking. I had at the time thought it a bit redundant to teach a Basset Hound, whose sense of smell was a million times better than any human's and a thousand times more accurate than any other breed of dog, how to track using his nose. But we learned that although he had a great sense of smell, he did need to learn how to use it properly. Now was a good time to prove how effective that training really was.

"Do you have anything with the scent of the rabbits on it?" I asked Dan and Mary.

"Straw from their cage?" Mary asked expectantly, snuffling her nose on the sleeve of her sweatshirt.

"Perfect."

"I'll run back and get some," she exclaimed. "Our house is just off the path. I'll be back in flash, Dad!" And off she ran to fetch a bit of bunny bedding.

While we waited, Dan told me about the two rabbits.

"Actually, they're purebred European hares. Lepus europaeus..." he explained.

".. of the family Leporidae[5]," I said.

"Yes, that's right."

"But they're indigenous to this area. Why are you keeping them in captivity?"

---

[5] Family of rabbits, of which there are more than eight known species.

"Mary's uncle raised rabbits to sell as pets for a hobby. Gave Huckleberry and Blueberry to her a few years ago as Easter presents. I don't think they would know how to fend for themselves in the wild, even if it is just in these small woods."

"Whoooo-hooowwwol!" Frankie said. "Owl."

"I think these woods have more in them than we think," I offered. "Like owls, and perhaps a fox or two. Here's hoping Frankie can find them in time."

It didn't take Mary long to return with a handful of dirty straw, as well as a large cloth cat carrier. "Just in case we find them," she said. I shoved the straw under Frankie's nose and commanded him to "Sniff", which he did. Twice; panting through his nose each time. He then let out a long, low whine and began to strain on the leash, pulling me down the path, his nose scouring the ground.

"I think he's 'on the line'!" I called back, trailing after Frankie, holding on to the end of the lease for dear life. "He's picked up their scent! Tally-ho!"

Frankie bounded on ahead down the path for a few yards, then stopped, circled, and sniffed both the ground and the gentle evening breezes. As he circled, his white-tipped tail stood straight up, feathering[6] the air. He sniffed left, then right, then left again. Then he raised his head, panted a few times so that air puffed out of his mouth, fluttering his flews, then dropped his snout to sniff the ground again. He repeated this pattern for a few minutes, until he was sure of the scent. And then, suddenly, barely lifting his head, he "woofed" and again charged off the path toward the creek.

I had a hard time keeping up with him, holding on to my end of his lead. Dan and Mary, however, had no trouble jogging alongside me. At this brisk pace, the three of us followed him to a copse of overgrown azalea bushes, at least 100 feet from the path, at the end of a sharp turn in the creek. A patch of wild strawberries encircled the bushes. Here, the creek water was not as wide or deep, and branches of the bushes splayed out over the ripples. Whoever was tending these woods near our development had overlooked these shrubs or had not yet gotten around to trimming them.

Frankie sniffed the ground, howled, and then plunged under the lowest branches, scrambling around in the dirt, letting out his usual "I found it!" series of short,

---

[6] A hunting term. When a hound feathers his tail, it means he has picked up the scent and is "on the line".

guttural whines and "woofs" that barely escaped his flews. We also heard a series of high pitched squeaks and squeals.

"There is something in there, besides your dog," Dan offered. "If he's done his job, that's got to be Huckleberry and Blueberry."

"Okay, Frankie," I said almost totally out of breath, pulling his lead and reaching for his collar. After a bit of difficulty struggling with the stubborn hound—there was no way he was going to lose sight of his prey---I finally dragged him out from under the shrubs. "Time to let us humans see what is there, big guy."

And there, huddled together under the azaleas, were two small, cringing rabbits, with mottled and matted fur. Each sported a thin, powder blue cat collar. They were shivering, obviously frightened, but made no attempt to flee. Instead, they sat very still, as if frozen.

Frankie, now sitting expectantly by my side, was still straining to get at the rabbits. I suspect that since Basset Hounds were bred to primarily hunt and slay rabbits, he thought that since he found them, he was entitled to them.

"No, not tonight, big guy," I said. "Finding rabbits with your great nose is one thing. Trying to eat them is another. That is not allowed, especially when they are someone's pets!"

I shortened his lead and grasped his collar tightly, holding him back, while, with great care, Dan and Mary managed to corral the still squealing Huckleberry and Blueberry into the cat carrier.

"It's okay," Mary tried to soothe them. "They're safe now, Daddy. Why are they still so frightened?"

"Woof!" Frankie said.

"I think," I translated, "they're trying to tell you what happened."

And, once again, with Frankie as translator, the two bunnies told their short tale.

That afternoon, a rogue raccoon had ventured out of the woods and onto the deck and managed to unhitch the latch of the rabbit hutch. Curious as all rabbits are, when the raccoon scurried off, the two pets pushed open the door, hopped out, and began to explore. Before they knew it, they had ventured off the porch, onto the path, and into the woods where, lured by the scent of the wild strawberries, promptly got lost. Frightened by the strange noises coming from the woods around them, they hid under the azaleas.

"And, so, here they are, safe and sound again," I said.

"Thank you, Frankie, for finding them," Mary said, patting his head.

"Woofie-woof-woof!. You are entirely welcome!"

"I think we've had enough adventure for one night's walk. Let's head back home," I suggested, leading Frankie back to the path. Dan picked up the cat carrier and took Mary's hand.

The sun now set behind the trees, the three of us, with our cherished pets in hand, amiably walked back together to our townhomes, following the path by the light of the new, harvest moon, just rising over French Creek. After saying "Good evening" to Dan and Mary and the two European hares at the foot of their deck, I let Frankie off-lead again. He, of course, quickly bounded ahead of me eagerly anticipating his nightly biscuit and curling up on his rumpled blanket on the foot of my bed to revel in his own thoughts and dreams.

He didn't have much to say for the rest of the evening as we had our dinner and then prepared for bed, except to say, "Now, that was a fun walk! Can we do it again sometime?"

"Yes," I said. "I am sure we will walk together again many, many more times."

And, so, we did. And each one, I assure you, was, indeed, with Frankie One, a great adventure unto itself.

MY HERO, FRANKIE

Frankie, my first Bassett Hound had a mind of his own. His laid back countenance hid a super intelligence. Like most members of his breed, this was masked by his eagerness to spend most of his time slumbering anywhere. The sofa, a big chair, his own recliner in the bedroom. The original couch chewie, he was loath to move. Nothing moved or shook him when he was prone—except for a whiff of grilling steak, the word "Biscuit", or the cat saucily sauntering by (just to annoy him). Any one of these would instantly rouse him into action: alert, barking, and quickly chasing down whatever disturbed his peace. Any other attempt to touch him when he was sleeping would have resulted in a quick nip and an annoyed growl.

For years, I had thought only food and the cat would rouse him. I never thought that protecting his territory and his mistress would ever be primary. While I originally got a dog for protection, Frankie never exhibited this trait; it was never one of his finer points. After a few years of trying to convince myself he would become a good guard dog, I gave up and contended myself with his friendly, often humorous companionship and what I thought was a decidedly lazy nature.

Our companionship grew into mutual contentment. He was friendly to all. His life's ambition was to sit, or sleep, on the sunniest side of the road and be a friend to (wo)man. After ten short years, I thought this was always going to be true.

Until one cool March evening when he was ten…

We were having an après-dinner nap together on the couch before our evening walk. Frankie snuggled warmly in the hollow of my curled legs, as we peacefully slumbered together, while soft, early evening breezes wafted through the opened kitchen sliding glass doors to the deck...

Half awake, I thought I heard a shout outside. Or was it the rustle of the remnants of last winter's unraked leaves? A faint light across the lawn from the distance moved and angled into the window. Was I dreaming?

"Did you hear that, big guy?" I asked, scratching behind his velvet ear. Still sound asleep, Frankie growled softly, and then snapped wide awake. I braced for the warning nip. Instead, he sat upright, lifted his tri-colored snout for a quick sniff, and then propelled off the sofa into the kitchen. Pawing angrily at the screen door, he ripped the black mesh to shreds and bounded onto the deck and out into the yard.

Annoyed that I had been awakened so rudely, I yawned, grumbled a few choice words, grabbed Frankie's lead and the flashlight from the kitchen counter, and shuffled out onto the deck.

A menacing-looking man dressed in dark navy blue stood frozen in my yard. His flashlight aimed into Frankie's eyes, who stood rigidly in front of him, barking loudly. My light beamed into the man's face. In its shadow, the bulge under his jacket was a holstered gun in his belt.

I waffled between letting Frankie fend for himself or to go back inside to call 911—a dark stranger in the middle of the evening in my backyard is not a safe situation—or accosting the intruder.

"Is this your dog?" He asked, reaching down to pet Frankie. "Is he friendly?"

"Yes, he is. To friendly people." I gruffly responded. Frankie was the friendliest dog on the block; in the whole neighborhood. Perhaps the town. Him aggressive? Hardly. Only when rudely awoken; only when playing with me.

Frankie sat at attention, accepting the attention, suddenly eager to please.

"Who are you?" I asked, puzzled that I had never seen Frankie act this way before.

"Police," he said, flashing a bronze badge pinned inside his jacket on his shirt pocket. "The Acme has been robbed. Two young men with knives made off with a plastic shopping bag full of money. They were spotted running toward your house. Have you seen them?"

"No, we were napping." I snapped Frankie's lead on and started walking back to our deck. "Hope you catch them soon."

"You and your dog should stay inside until we do," the policeman said. "The older one punched the cashier, and then stabbed her arm. No telling what he will do if someone else gets in his way. My partner and I are searching the area. We're thinking both of them are hiding by the creek. I'm on my way there now. "

When the policeman left, I swept my flashlight's beam across the yard and my deck stairs to ensure no one else was around. I started to lead Frankie back into the house, but he refused to come in. Instead, he growled and strained at the collar as I tried to restrain him and bring him to my side. The closer I got, the more he pulled backwards. Finally, he defiantly barked and snipped, squeezed out of his collar, and began to eagerly sniff the ground. He stopped briefly at the edge of my neighbor's deck, looked up at me, then bounded after the policemen, howling his best hound-on-the-scent "whooo-ooo-oooo".

I watched in astonishment. He had never acted like this before. I yelled "Frankie, NO!" a few times, but to no avail. Like a true Basset, he was totally focused on one thing; obeying me wasn't it. I was too afraid to leave the deck lest I, too, be attacked by the young knife-wielding robber. Frankie rushed back to my neighbor's deck, howled at it, then scampered back to the policeman. It was evident he was trying to say something.

The policemen chuckled, "No time to play now, boy. I gotta go." He hastened further away as Frankie made his fourth trip back to the deck next door, and then disappeared under it.

A long, silent moment.

Where was he? Was he alright? I stepped off the deck. I heard a piercing, ear-splitting whine.

A loud yelp!

Then total silence.

I panicked.

"Frankie?!" I shouted. "Come out, big guy. Are you alright?"

The silence continued.

Finally, his low rumbling shaken-from-the-sofa slumber growl emanated from the darkness under the deck.

He's probably trapped, I thought. Though I had no desire to crawl under after him, I knew I had to help him. He was such a gentle hound. He had no experience in this kind of situation. I eased my way to the edge of the deck, and scanned the gaping hole under it with my flashlight.

"Frankie? Are you under there? Are you okay?"

Red hair, orange tee-shirt, and ripped blue jeans suddenly flashed out at me. A knife in one hand, plastic bag in the other, a young man, screaming at the top of his lungs, nearly ran me over, bumped into my deck railing, veered to his right, and headed towards the bushes at the back edge of my yard.

"Get him off me! Get him off me!"

Frankie's mouth was stalwartly clamped onto his jeans seat; his lower body dangling, rear paws barely touching the ground.

"Police!" I yelled loudly. "Police!"

The young robber. screaming at the top of his lungs, doubled over into the bushes, with growling Frankie firmly attached to his backside. His swung his knife wildly, barely missing Frankie's neck with each swipe.

I screamed again, but the robber screamed even louder.

"Get him off me! Get him off me!"

Despite his clamp on the boy's rump, Frankie seemed to growl louder!

When the policemen finally arrived, running back from the creek, Frankie was standing on the young man's legs, his front paws squarely pinned in the middle of his back, holding him down with all his might. And teeth.

'We got him, now." the police said. "Drop the knife, son!"

"Get him off me! I'm afraid of dogs," He sobbed.

"Drop the knife and we'll call off the dog."

"Get him off me. Please."

"Drop the knife!"

"Call off your dog!" the officer yelled back at me, when the knife was finally dropped.

This was one command we never had to learn. "How do I do that?"

"Call *off* your dog!" he commanded again, handcuffing the boy. Frankie continued to growl.

In my best authoritative alpha-dog owner voice I shouted, "Frankie! Off!" Not knowing what he would do.

Pause.

No response.

Then I yelled "COME!" The only command besides "Go lie down" he's ever eagerly responded to.

Frankie instantly stopped growling. His jaws still firmly clamped blue jeans; he turned his head slightly with a hang-dog look, as if to say, "What do you want? Can't you see I'm a little busy right now?"

He paused.

And as if he did it a million times each day of his life—this was, in fact, the first time—he dropped the jeans, scrambled off the boy's back, "woofed!" at the policemen, and promptly heeled by my left side, snapping to attention.

He beamed, knowing exactly what he had just done. He strutted in place, pawing the ground, aware how proud of him I was; and he of himself.

"Good boy!" Dumbfounded, I cheered and petted his head. I had never seen him act like this before. What a good dog! Finally, he was the guard dog I had always wanted.

Or was he?

One policeman dragged the culprit away; the other asked where Frankie was trained to guard.

"He'd be a great addition to the force!"

"He wasn't trained to do this. Just obedience school—first level. He's just my companion."

"Comes naturally, huh?"

I agreed. I didn't know what else to say.

"He's got a gift. Not many of our well-trained police dogs can capture criminals like this one! Sure would like him to work with us. He'd make you proud."

"No thanks. He's happy just being my companion. Aren't you, Frankie?" I stroked his muzzle as he leaned and chortled into my hand.

"Hey, I did a good thing," he seemed to say. "And I know it!"

"We're proud of him just the way he is," I added.

"You're lucky he can protect you," the policeman said, scratching Frankie's head and patting his back. "You chose him well for that!"

"One of the perks of having a good dog. Right, Frankie?"

But having saved the day, and having gotten all the praise and attention a brave canine deserves, Frankie had other, more important things to do. He sniffed his good-byes, and ambled up the deck stairs into the house. Bounding onto the couch, he pawed and circled three times before curling up and sighing into its soft cushions. His sole intent at that moment was to continue his evening nap that was so abruptly interrupted.

Once he was settled in, I proudly, tentatively patted his brow, and then settled in next to him. He feigned a gently nip, growled softly for a while, and then promptly fell asleep. Probably dreaming of his next capture—true to his calling.

My hero.

FRANKIEB: IN HIS OWN WORDS

They brought me home in a brown and tan plaid blanket the second day of the New Year. At eight weeks, I was already a hefty twelve pounds, with a white, chunky, bullish body, saddled in mahogany, with tan ticks speckling my white shoulders and snout.

They named me "FrankieBernard" or "FrankieB" after their first Basset Hound, although I was a bit dismayed to learn that I wasn't the first "Frankie" in the house, but the second. My predecessor wasn't "FrankieA", just "Frankie".

Then I discovered that "they", the older couple and the younger woman were not to be my new family, as I had first thought, but just the younger one. The elderly, tall man with the silvery hair who cradled me in his arms during the long car ride from the kennel to here and the older woman with golden short hair had left a few, short hours after he carried me into the house wrapped in that plaid blanket. I was summarily left in a black-barred crate under a kitchen counter called a "breakfast bar" while the younger female fussed around the house cleaning up dishes and champagne glasses and spreading what I soon learned to be newspapers on the ground, er, the tile floor in front of me.

An orange cat occasionally jumped over the baby gate straddling the kitchen doorway and sniffed my cage. He mewled at me softly, then jumped upon the counter over my head—I think he was going to eat dinner there. Well, at least, I thought, there was some semblance of animal company besides this too-efficient woman.

Thus were my first impressions of my new home. It certainly was very much unlike the stable stall covered in straw in the huge, drafty barn where my mom, Harriet, had whelped me and my seven other siblings. And it was certainly different than what I had imagined would be my family—no scruffy children to corral, no backyard to romp in, and no other adult humans to cajole for an extra biscuit or two before dinner.

I was the fifth in line, or so the blue tattoo in my right ear attests. "42-4-5" it says—forty-second litter of the breeder that year, "4" being the number of my mother's fourth litter, and "5", my ranking in the birth order. Two others, I think, died before me. But I made it, a healthy, hale and hearty male Basset Hound puppy—soon destined to be...well, at that point, I wasn't sure what.

I have since learned from listening to conversations between my mistress and her various friends that where I live now, the homeowners association had a silly, strict one-pet rule that also limited the size of animals. She had promised that her first "Frankie", after whom I was named, would be perennially on a diet to try to conform to the maximum twenty-five pounds. But, at forty-five pounds, he just didn't quite make the grade. They had moved into the new house before the real estate agent and the then property manager brought my new mistress the rules and regulations. Frankie—now dubbed "FrankieA" after his demise eight years later—was already ensconced as a neighborhood mascot and much beloved by all he met. And so, acknowledging the error, the HOA board condescended to let him be kept by my new owner. When "Frankie" moved on to the Rainbow Bridge at the tender age of sixteen and a half (that's 108.5 in dog years[7]), and she had finally after a short two months decided to acquire another Basset Hound, my name, of course, had to be "Frankie" in deference to the first. And thus I became "FrankieBernard " or, as many neighbors have since dubbed me, "FrankieB", for short.

When I arrived, as I mentioned, there was already another animal in the house. A cream-colored tabby cat, a *feline*, whose name I soon learned was "Sebastian"—SabbyCat or, as my new owner was fond of calling him, "Kitty-Kat" (hard "Ks.", soft "a").

Apparently, he was the king of the walk, the pride of the household, and strutted around the house as if he owned the place...until I was carried into the door of the house wrapped in the plaid blanket by the older man and placed gently on the tiled kitchen floor. It was all Sebastian had to see—another intruder. But he was

[7] Dog years, according to the American Kennel Club (AKC) are calculated by counting the first year of a dog's age in human years as one and then adding the product of multiplying the remaining age in human years by seven. Thus, a dog who is six in human years, is actually thirty-six in dog years [1 + (5 x 7) = 36].

pretty blasé about it. Even at the tender age of eight weeks and one day, he pretty much ignored me if I didn't bother him too much. Which I didn't. I sensed I was about to make a new friend for life.

At the time, Sebastian and I weighed the same and were approximately the same size. But, still, as a fledgling puppy having not yet acquired any worldly ways, I was no match for his vast already three or four years experience as a proven hunter—apparently he was feral before adopting our mistress---and now as an established house cat. The second or third full day I was "at home", he asserted his authority by jumping over the gate onto the kitchen floor where I was busy sniffing the papers and getting acclimated to my new surroundings.

Rather than jump up onto the counter this time, he stood in the middle of the pile of newspapers and mewled loudly. I stood stock-still on my white paws, which were quite large for my small, chunky body. I walked a little clumsily on them—they would take a bit of getting used to as I grew into them. Anyway, there I was—cornered by the cat. So I did what any frightened puppy would do in this situation. I whimpered. Loudly. I am not sure if that surprised Sebastian, but he looked at me in such a way that my whimpering was not what he had expected. So, in deference, so he "told" me later, he sidled up to me and rubbed his whole body against mine, purring just as loudly as I whimpered.

Hearing the caterwauling and whines from the kitchen, our mistress got up from her desk in the family room and peered into the kitchen to see what was going on.

"Play nice, guys" was all she said. "You're both going to be living together here for a long time, so just accept it and get along."

It was the beginning of our beautiful friendship.

After I was properly trained and housebroken, and no longer had to be confined in the kitchen all the time by the baby gates, I was allowed to freely roam and explore the house. Sometimes Sebastian and I roamed and explored together. Other times, I ambled around by myself, testing my legs and running back and forth up and down the stairs—sounding like a ten-pound bowling ball thundering down a warped alley—while my mistress sat at her desk (she called it "working") while Sebastian took one of his many, daily catnaps on our mistress' big bed; an orange fur ball curled up upon the beige and green eiderdown quilt.

One of our favorite activities together was looking out the front storm door at the neighborhood, watching the birds and squirrels flit and scurry across the lawn, expecting people to walk by, and cringing at the loud belching coming from the garbage trucks that passed by every other day.

My favorite person to amble by on the sidewalk with his father or older sister was little Miguel. He was less than two years old when I arrived on the scene and was introduced to him as both of us were held by our respective "parents"—I in my mistress' arms and he in his father's.

"Look at the puppy," Miguel's Dad said.

"Coo," said Miguel.

I barked a hearty "WOOF! ARF! ARF!" which, at first, frightened the little tyke, but then, as I softened my voice into my own puppy whimpers and coos, he smiled and laughed, stretching out his hands and wiggling his fingers at me. It became our special code for "HI, Miguel!" and "Hiya, FrankieB!" Soon, we were both allowed to play together on the carpet in what I now consider "my" living room when Miguel's parents and older siblings visited. Miguel was fascinated by my squeaky toys, which he carried around, tossing them at me. I think he thought I would fetch them for him, but I am not that sort of hound. I'll find them for him if he hides them, yes; but fetch them for him? I think not. Still, it provided hours of captivating play for both of us. We both became so attuned to one another—so much so that whenever he and I are both around, we are inseparable. Gosh, how I have come to love that kid.

It was shortly after I was finally housebroken that I was allowed to sleep with Sebastian and our mistress in her big bed. These are the best times of the day, the late evenings, all curled up together, snuggling under the covers, all warm and tight — especially on chilly autumn or snowy winter nights. That same time I began to call my mistress "Mom", for that is what I now call her. After all, she does take care of me much in the same way Miguel's parents take care of him. Anyway, I love the scent of lavender soap that lingers on her cheek and neck after her bedtime shower, and when I am curled up in my own mahogany ball close by her side, the way she massages the back of my neck, just behind the ears when she softly says, "Good night, sweet FrankieBernard. Sleep well." She pets Sebastian, too, in the same way, I guess. But he sleeps stretched out on her other side and my eyes are closed shut, enjoying my massage, so I can't see him and don't really know.

One day in mid-October, a few years after coming into my new home, we were all on the back deck, lounging in the warm rays of the early afternoon sun. I had just had my usual long walk around the neighborhood with Mom. Sebastian had awoken from his after-lunch catnap, and Mom had fixed herself a tuna fish sandwich, which she was going to munch while reading a book. The deck is really a small balcony with French doors leading onto it from the family room. It's two stories up, overlooking our driveway, a back alley, a strip of woods with a stream, and a road beyond.

In the fall, when the leaves start to drop from the trees in the woods, and the migratory geese honk overhead on their way south, there is enough space between the branches so that we can see the traffic that zooms up and down the road and the buses that stop near the entrance to our neighborhood. There are three bus stops: one for school buses, and one on either side of the road for the SEPTA buses. The two or three school buses come once each in the afternoon. But the SEPTA buses stop at least twice every hour in their travels to and fro beyond our small village to the city, various other towns, shopping malls, train stations, and a myriad of other bus stops, carrying all sorts of people back and forth, hither and yon.

I really love to settle next to Mom on warm, sunny days with my huge front paws draped over the arm of the small wicker settee, my ears perked up (as much as a Basset Hound's ears could perk) listening to the sounds all around me, with my eyes peeled over the railing to watch the buses. Since Mom and I walk the neighborhood at least once, sometimes twice, daily, I've gotten to know just about everyone (and just about everyone has gotten to know me); and I've gotten to know just about everybody who gets on and off both the school and SEPTA buses at our stops.

I remember it was Friday. I was almost four (that's twenty-two in dog years), and Sebastian was going on five or six (thirty-six or forty in human years[8]). He was crouched down low, with his body squeezed half-way through the vertical bars, his head and tabby-cat paws draped over the edge of the balcony. As I said, I was on the wicker settee guarding Mom, who had finished her tuna sandwich and had opened her book, with my ears perked and eyes alert. This, I had come to assume, was

---

[8] Sebastian's age is according to the calculations on cats.about.com.

my daily job, besides snoozing on the tufted couch in the afternoons—guarding her while she read or "worked".

The red and white SEPTA bus stopped and its doors hissed open to let out two people, a man and a woman, whom we had never seen before. Like I said, I know just about everyone who comes and goes around here and that couple, that brace[9] of people, was definitely *not* from around here.

As they stepped off the bus, I took special note of what they were wearing. The man had on black corduroy slacks, a pink Oxford-cloth shirt, and a loose-fitting black-and-tan plaid blazer. He wore high-top Nike sneakers on his feet, and a black felt fedora on his head. In his right hand, he carried a gnarled cane—what you might call, I later learned, a shillelagh—and in his left hand, a small, brown, leather valise. The woman was similarly garbed in black jeans, a pink blouse, and a brown cardigan sweater that sagged almost to her knees. Her purse was a large, bulging messenger bag; its wide strap slung crisscross over her shoulders and chest. She, too, carried a small, brown, leather valise.

---

[9] A "brace" is a hunting term for a pair of hounds, usually coupled together by leads.

After descending from the bus, whose doors hissed closed behind then, they sauntered almost aimlessly to the entrance of our development, turned into it, and then paused to check their watches and consult an index card that the man pulled from his inside jacket pocket. Then they walked up the alley and stopped at the foot of our driveway.

At that point, I began to bark and howl. Loudly. Fiercely. I made enough noise to alert the whole neighborhood.

Who were these people? Why were they here?

For all I knew, they were intruders, robbers come to divest us of all our worldly treats, er, goods—my favorite chewy treats and gravy-coated biscuits, not to mention SabbyCat's plush mice stuffed with catnip! Then my Basset's friendly nature took the better of me—I've never met a stranger I didn't like and who didn't, finally, become my friend—and I softened my barks and howls down to grunting bays and whimpering; as if to say, "Welcome, who are you? Who are you? Have you come to play with me?"

Mom continued to read, ignoring me and the strangers until she had finished the page she was on.

Finally, she looked up and tried to silence me, but all I could do was howl and bark, then bay and grunt and whimper, while the couple stood upon the apron of our driveway, looking up at us. Sebastian, on the other hand, at the very onset of my vocal renditions, promptly ran into the house, probably to hide under the couch or a bed. He was good like that in the face of uncertainty.

A bemused and somewhat cynical smile crossed the man's face. I could see he was rather young, at least younger than Mom. The woman was more somber-looking. She smoothed her wavy, red hair, tinged with grey, back into a long ponytail, rewrapped its elastic band, and frowned. They waited patiently for Mom to calm me down. It took at least two liver treats and a chewy until I was quiet enough so that she could finally speak and be heard.

"May I help you?" she asked, standing up to lean over the rail, her book in hand.

"We're not sure if we're in the right place," the man answered in what was, to me, an unfamiliar, strange accent. "We're looking for June."

"I'm June," Mom said. "Who are you?"

"We're your distant cousins. I am Steve and this is my wife, Peg. We've come to visit and deliver a message."

"That's a fine-looking hound," Peg said. "What's his name?"

"Woofie-Woof!" I said.

"FrankieBernard," Mom translated. "FrankieB, for short."

"And so he is," the woman quipped. "You can call me 'Peggy'."

"Where did you say you were from?" Mom queried again.

Steve cleared his throat, then raised his shillelagh, as if to tout his origins.

"Ireland. County Clare. Of the Mac an Airchinnigh[10] Clan," he called up. "They were your ancestors. May we come in for a spot of tea and a visit?"

Now, Mom and I are not ones to let just anyone into the house, but there was something I sensed Mom feeling about Peggy and Steve, that was kind and nice

[10] Pronounced "mock-on-arc-kenny".

and wonderful. And so, with great haste, she directed them around the side of the house to the front door, where she greeted them with a warm smile and a brisk shake of each one's hand.

"Come in, Mac an Airchinnighs of County Clare, Ireland," she said, ushering them into the family room. "Please make yourselves at home while I make some tea. You must have had a long journey."

Steve instantly commandeered the large recliner in the corner by the fireplace, where Sebastian normally took his early evening nap, while Peggy arranged herself daintily on one end of the couch. I, of course, couldn't resist jumping up next to her and sniffing her ears and mouth, begging for attention and back scratches, if I could get them. I wasn't so sure about Steve, yet. Getting to know him would come later that evening. While Mom made tea and scrounged around for some human biscuits to serve with them, SabbyCat perched upon his breakfast bar counter, aloofly surveying the whole scene.

"I don't normally invite strangers into my home," Mom said, carrying in a large, wooden tray laden with teapot, mugs, spoons, a pitcher of milk, a small jar of saccharine—sugar is not allowed in our house—and a small plate of buttered scones left over from last Christmas. I could smell that they weren't stale, thank goodness, having been in the cupboard for almost a year. That would have been embarrassing to Mom, and distasteful to me, because I knew I was going to get a crumb or two from our guests.

"I understand," Peg said. "We don't usually enter strange homes. Here, let me help you," she said, rising to take the tray from Mom and place it on the low table before us as Mom cleared it of stacks of books, newspapers, and Wii game DVDs. "Shall I pour?"

Mom acquiesced and then asked a myriad of questions while the humans sipped their hot tea and nibbled the scones. I anxiously sat at attention, listening and drooling, waiting for a treat. One of the cardinal rules of dogdom, of which there are many, is that if you stare at something long enough, you'll eventually get what you want.

How were they related? Why had they come to visit? Have they been in the United States long? What is the message they have come to give? How long were they staying? Where were they staying?

"We were hoping," Steve said in his thick, Irish brogue—that strange, funny accent of his—draining the last of his tea and looking shyly into his empty mug, "that we might stay with you, June, and dear FrankieB here." I had finally sidled up to him and sat at attention by his leg, while he reached down to rub my head.

"Me? And FrankieB?" Mom asked incredulously. "Why, it's one thing to ask strangers in for tea. It's quite another to have them stay overnight for breakfast!"

"But we're no strangers, lass," Peggy said. "Remember, we're of the clan Mac an Airchinnigh, our, your ancestors. We've no place else to go, having not been able to find a suitable inn around here. And we won't be much trouble, I promise."

"I am not so sure," Mom said, clearing away the tea dishes and scone crumbs. That was her signal that the visit was over and it was time for Steve and his helpful wife to leave. "I am not one to take in the homeless...someone with 'no place else' to go."

"We're not homeless. At least not in Ireland," Peg responded. "We've a lovely home in County Clare, very much like your own, with our own dog, Lucie, who just happens to be a purebred Basset, just like Frankie. It's just that in our haste to get here, we were a little short-sighted when planning the trip."

I woofed when she said "Basset". They have a Basset Hound? Like me? Named "Lucie"? What were the odds? Why didn't she come along with them? I would have loved to have met my "cousin".

"Why didn't you call or email first?" Mom queried. "My contact information is on my Web site."

"We were concerned you might think it would be spam or one of those money scams that are so rampant on the Internet," Peggy explained. "We thought it best to do this in person. Besides, we've never been to the States and we did need a bit of a vacation. So, dearie, here we are."

"Listen," Steve said, reaching into his valise and pulling out a sheaf of papers, "I ought to tell you that I am a developer in County Clare—I buy tracts of land and build homes, mostly townhome communities with shopping centers and such on them, and then sell the units and rent the store space."

"He's made a good living for us both, and Lucie, of course," Peg smiled. She took one last bite out of her scone and passed the last bit of it on to me. See? Staring works!

What good people these two are turning out to be!

Mom's anxiety seemed to ease at hearing about Steve's vocation. She settled back onto the couch next to Peg to hear more of their story.

"We, you and I," Steve continued, "as you know, are direct descendants of Vincent McInerney who left County Clare in 1862 and came to the States during your Civil War. There are no more records about him in Ireland...I had to search the Internet to find out what happened to him. I found a site with your research from two years ago, listing his descendants, you and your parents and your brother among them."

"Yes, that's right," Mom said, vigorously rubbing me behind my ears. "I couldn't find anything before1862 about him. Like how he came to America and where he came from in Ireland."

"Here are copies of those records," Steve said, handing them to Mom. "There is also a copy of his father's will. They should answer your question."

Mom ruffled through the papers and found sepia-toned papers stapled together. I sniffed and caught the faint scent of musk and old copier toner. I could tell that in them was, indeed, a tale to tell, much longer than my own white-tipped, er, tail. The reproduction of early nineteenth century writing was pale and fading, at best. It took her a while to read the writing patterns with the ornate serifs.

"Well, at least it's in English," she said. "What I can make of it is, anyway. Let's see what it says." She paused to peer at the will. "It says that he leaves what remains of his 'fortune' to his only son and heir, Vincent, and, if not claimed, to his, Vincent's, direct descendants.

"Well, why didn't Vincent claim it?" Mom asked.

"Because the family lived poorly after the Great Potato Famine of 1845 and, thinking he was poor, Vincent left for America," Steve explained. "Because of the Civil War, all communications between the States, both North and South, and Europe were interrupted and sparse, at best. He never learned of his father's death. And, obviously, the will was subsequently lost. Until a few weeks ago, when I found it."

Steve and Peggy went on to relate that Steve found the will while researching the title to a tract of land upon which he wanted to build one of his townhome complexes, complete with a strip mall, a recreation center, and a small chapel.

"The will turned up in an old book in the records room of the small parish church, where the tract of land is located. We weren't sure at first," he said, "who Vincent McInerney was, until Peg, here, researched his history further."

"And that's when we discovered that the 'fortune' is yours and ours," Peg said.

"So, what is it?" Mom asked.

"Well," Steve said, "it turns out that the tract of land, with the ruins of the Mac an Airchinnigh Castle on it belongs to us. It is, was, Vincent's inherited 'fortune' he could never claim and has passed on to us."

"A castle?" Mom asked, taken aback.

"Yes, given to one of our ancestors a long time ago by a King of England in gratitude for valiant behavior on the field of battle—that much we know. Nothing else. But here is the deed to prove it."

"My word," Mom said. "Is that the seal of Henry the VIII? I can't tell...it's a bit blurred. My word. Whatever are we going to do with a castle?"

"Ah, there's the rub," Steve said. "Vincent's father was unable to keep it up and fell behind in paying the taxes. He moved the family off the land into town, before Vincent was born, and never told his son about the castle, which was, by then, falling into great disrepair. So, we're a bit in debt to County Clare for the back levies. But if we develop the lots as I plan, then we can recoup the loss and make some money, besides."

"Enough so that we could all retire in style," Peg said.

I knew this was Mom's fondest dream, to retire from the boring job she was currently in and write her stories and spend long, languishing days with me and Sebastian.

However, skeptic that she sometimes is, she said, "It can't be." She paused. "Can it?"

"Let's work on that," Peg said, getting up and going into the kitchen. "If you don't mind, I think I'll clean up the tea things."

During the next few days, Steve and Peggy turned out to be, in my mind, wonderful additions to our household. We, Mom and I, showed them off to our neighbors and friends on what quickly became our twice daily walks—one in the early morning before breakfast (Peggy and Steve, much to my Mom's chagrin, were early risers), and one in the early evening before dinner. I showed them my favorite grassy areas where I gather my "smell mail" and do my "stuff". Now, isn't that what life is all about? Eat, sniff, poop!

In the mornings after breakfast, if there weren't any errands to run in town, they would gather in the family room and discuss their plans for the new Castle Keep development on the old Mac an Airchinnigh lands. Steve used Mom's desk in the corner to design the layout of the development and to draw up plans for the many townhomes and village shops he would build.

Steve also became quickly accustomed to the big recliner, usurping Sebastian in the early evenings, claiming it and the corner as his "man space", relaxing and sipping his tea, reading the evening newspaper, listening to the women chattering away or playing Scrabble©. In the later part of the evenings, after dinner, if it was chilly enough, Mom and Steve would build a fire to heat up the downstairs and the humans would gather around it to share stories of past and present lives, sharing some of their Irish heritage and traditions. Sebastian and I, of course, during these gatherings, found our own new spots on the couch between Mom and Peggy and on the red chair against the wall between the kitchen and the main hallway. We listened with great interest to the humans talk.

Our short days and evenings together were peaceful, yet full of the many warm feelings and adventures that close friends and relatives have when they come together to visit.

One morning, we took Peggy and Steve to the ritzy doggie day care center[11] that I used to attend when Mom had to work in the office. Peggy and Steve weren't sure what a "day care" center was until it was explained to them.

"Ach," Peggy said. "A nursery for dogs; what we call a 'crèche'—a canine crèche," she giggled, laughing at her own joke, She was so impressed with the heated, salinated pool, the clean yards that were sodded with

---

[11] Wagsworth Manor, Malvern, PA. "The luxury retreat for the furry elite." www.wagsworth.com.

doggie astro-turf, and the amiable staff, that she decided Castle Keep would have a pet crèche, too.

While they took the tour, I had a chance to romp with some of my buddies whom I hadn't seen in a while;: Twinkle, the miniature poodle, who also lived in our neighborhood; Butch, the Bulldog, who loved to stand atop the plastic playground ramp and bark at the other dogs below; and Dolly, the Basset Hound, who shared the picture with me on the poster for a local shelter. It was indeed a glorious, brilliant[12] morning, playing and rolling in the grass with all my old friends!

Then we went to the dog park near the big shopping center on the other side of town. Since it was a weekday and most people were working, there weren't very many dogs there; and so, it wasn't much fun for me, except that Albert, a lively, very tall Labradoodle was there, and he let me run under his belly and around his legs for a bit, while Peg and Mom and Steve checked out the layout of the place. I knew they were thinking of duplicating the park, too, in their new development. Castle Keep was really going to be dog-friendly!

---

[12] This is the Irish euphemism for our word, "grand".

Our last stop that morning was the pet store, where I was allowed to roam the aisles and select my favorite treats and dog food. Mom bought a huge bag of kibble for me and a case of tuna surprise for Sebastian. Steve bought a few of the gravy-coated biscuits that I so love to have after my walks, and stuck them into his pocket for us, er, me to share later.

He was turning out to be, in my mind, a really neat guy, even though he did commandeer Sebastian's resting place.

Steve told me more about their own Basset Hound, Lucie, who had golden, amber eyes and more of a brown coat, with less white showing then I. He explained that it would have been too much of a hassle to take her on the big jumbo jet that brought him and Peggy here, what with all the paper work they would have had to do to prove she had all her shots. And then there was the possibility of a long quarantine in a government kennel before she was allowed into the States. He also didn't like the idea of her having to ride for five hours in an unpadded crate in the cargo bay of a plane, either. It was far better, and much more comfortable, for Lucie to stay with Peggy's sister, Linda, on her small farm outside of Knockalough, where she and her husband raised sheep. Lucie, I imagined, would have a good time learning to herd—another of our little-known, but little used, Basset talents. Steve said he and Peg lived in Eignough[13], on the mouth of the River Shannon[14].

That evening by the fire, Peggy and Steve told Mom about her other Irish relatives—her cousins and great-aunts and uncles, who, as Peggy said, "were no longer with us, but still alive in our hearts and memories, just the same." The best story was their Christmas tradition of making "Mock Goose" each year. She explained it was "four pounds of steak made tender by beating and rubbing with lemon juice. After sewing the pieces up to form a big pocket," like that of a real goose or turkey, it was filled with bread, "sage and onion stuffing" and roasted with "sausages and served with sauces and vegetables just as though it was a roast goose"[15]. I couldn't help but slobber at the thought of all those rich aromas filling up our home on Christmas Day. Mom said

---

[13] Pronounced "egg-nog" "egg-knock," "ere-nog," or "ere-knock", depending upon where you're from.

[14] I suspect, if you're really curious, you will look these places up in an atlas. The village of Eignough, based upon a combination of real Irish villages, is fictitious.

[15] This recipe is originally from *Henderson's Quarterly Magazine,* 1910, and cited in *The Irish Christmas Book, ©1985,* edited by John Killen, The Blackstaff Press Limited, Belfast, Ireland.

she would try and make it for me this yuletide. I'm really looking forward to that this year! She promised!

The visit of Mom's cousins was almost like Christmas in itself. Each night, Mom and Peg made a scrumptious dinner, which we all gathered around the dining room table to eat. I can still picture them standing together side-by-side at the kitchen sink snapping green beans together, laughing and carrying on just like they were close sisters and not distant cousins. Once in awhile, we'd have apple pie with Hagen-Dazs vanilla ice cream—Mom's only concession to real sugar—and Steve would make steaming cups of Irish Coffee, topped with real whipped cream.

There was always laughter and good cheer, even though I sensed an undercurrent of seriousness. At some point, there was going to be lots of work to do.

After a few days, Steve announced that "we have to think about business". There was Vincent's father's estate, or what was left of it, to finally settle—even though the will was over 140 years old—and to figure out who was really going to inherit it, and what parts. He seemed anxious to get on with the work of developing the land and to reap the promised profits.

Peggy agreed, although she said she'd like to see the original castle restored.

"That will take lots of time and money," Steve said in a very matter-or-fact voice. "We have neither, at the moment. And June needs to decide whether to come back to Ireland with us and prove her claim to her share of the estate or stay here and be a 'silent, distant' partner."

"Oh, boy," I woofed. "Ireland! I can meet Lucie!"

Then I thought about the difficulty Steve said it would have been to bring Lucie to the States. How much more trouble would it be for me to travel to Ireland? And back again?

"Then there's the issue with my brother," Mom said. "He, too, is a direct descendant. Shouldn't he have a part in all of this, as well?"

"Yes," Steve said. "We've delayed long enough. I think we should call him."

And, that night, they did.

Uncle Rick was excited to hear about the possibility of an inheritance from an ancestor in a distant land. He, like Peggy, wanted to explore the possibility of restoring the castle. He said, though, that he didn't think he could make the trip, for whatever reasons, but that Mom should go.

"Rick said I should go back with you," Mom told Peggy and Steve. "He said it would do me 'a world of good'. Whatever that means."

"What about me?!? What about me?!?" I danced in anticipation around her legs as she stood by the French doors, cradling the phone in her ears looking out their windows across to the woods faintly lit by the sunset—and beyond.

"I supposed I could get the time off from work...put FrankieB in the Wagsworth kennels for a while. How long do you think the trip will take?"

"Well," said Steve, doing a bit of mental calculations. "It will take at least a few weeks to settle the estate—we'd all have to be there for that, the courts and all, you know, would want to see us in person. Then, well, however long it takes for us to finalize and file the plans for Castle Keep. Then, you and FrankieB can return home and come back again, once the development is finished and we have the grand opening."

"FrankieB? To Ireland?" Mom asked incredulously. She had heard the list of things Steve would have had to do just to bring Lucie here. Would it be worth it? Certainly, she couldn't leave me in the crèche, er, day care, as much as I would love it—weeks on end living and playing with my canine friends. But I would dearly miss Mom and I wanted so much to meet Lucie!

"I am not sure I can get that much time off," Mom said. "I've already used up most of my vacation and sick time. I don't think the company will think highly of my taking time off without benefit of pay, or any definite date of return."

"Then quit," Peggy said. "You've been talking of taking an early retirement ever since we got here. Now's your chance. We're bound to make money on this venture—enough, as I said, for all of us to retire."

"Townhouses sell like hotcakes in southern Ireland," Steve prompted. "How can we lose?"

"And," Peggy said, much like what I imagine an attorney would say in closing a case in court, "you can do your creative writing full-time, and not just piecemeal, like you've been doing. Think of the story this will be!"

And so it was decided that Mom would take a short leave of absence, and then take that early retirement she had dreamed so much about. More importantly, they all decided that I was to go with her to Ireland. The bottom line was that, of course, it would be far less expensive than boarding me at the fancy-Dan kennels for a month. Yeah! I would really get to meet and play with Lucie after all!

And that is how, after a whirlwind week of Mom getting her passport renewed and starting the paperwork so that her leave of absence[16] would take effect while she away and me going to the vet's to get all my shots and my documentation completed, and, of course, a quick trip to my favorite groomer at Hair of the Dog[17], I found myself in my own comfortable, padded crate in the passenger compartment of a Pets Express jet on my way to Shannon International Airport! Mom, Peggy, and Steve travelled, of course, on a big A330 Aer Lingus jumbo jet, in luxurious business class, no less. I heard later that they even got to sleep in their own assigned beds, and dined on fine china, and sipped their

---

[16] My mom's manager was not very happy with Mom's decision, but, then again, she was never happy or pleased with anything Mom did anyway, even though she is a great writer—so it really didn't matter.

[17] This is a really wonderful grooming salon—FrankieB's favorite. Check it out at www.hairofthedogphoenixville.com. Thanks, Jean!

drinks out of Waterford crystal glasses. Unfortunately, the airline did not accommodate pets or animals of any kind, for that matter, and, so, I had to travel by myself.

Well, not really by myself, per se, as the pet transport company picked me up at our house in a van and drove me to the airport, where I was greeted by a steward and two other dogs, who were also flying with me: a male Newfoundland named Boris and an elderly Irish Setter, Rusty. I didn't know if the humans were being taken care of as well as I during their flight, but I was treated royally, as I should be. After all, my pedigree does go back to the 1850s! There were in-cabin treats and fresh spring water, comfy pillows and fluffy, soft quilts to nap on, and even music piped in through overhead speakers to calm any nervous beast. There was no reason to be scared or to howl or bark, even at the whine of the twin jet engines. I wasn't and I didn't. What a good boy was I! When I arrived at the cargo area of Shannon International, there was Mom waiting to greet me with open arms, hugs, a long belly rub, and, of course, my favorite gravy-coated treats!

Am I spoiled, or what?

Sebastian, unfortunately, couldn't join us. He was boarded out to Mom's friends, Miguel's family. But I don't think he minded it. They have a black and grey tabby named Trevor, who, we were told later, thoroughly enjoyed SabbyCat's company.

Ireland, to say the least, is absolutely gorgeous. It took an hour or so for Steve to drive Mom and me from Shannon southwest down what I at first thought was the wrong side[18] of the N18 through lush, greener-than-green farm lands and heaths—I wanted so much to get out of the back of the car and go for a run—to the town square, called a "centre", with the most delightful red brick buildings trimmed in white, with lots of shops where we could buy almost anything. There was a marina, and a whole host of apartment buildings and townhomes—some newly developed, I suspect, by Steve—a few monuments to saints and martyrs to the Irish Rebellions, a theatre, and even a small opera house. Steve parked the car on Francis Street (hey, "Francis" is part of my AKC name, B'set Wizard Saint Francis) where I was properly introduced to the Clearey/McNamara hounds. These are hunting dogs, who "chase the hare" on Tuesday and Saturday mornings, although they also, occasionally, catch the scent of fox and go romping about that. A brace of them were lounging outside the hunt club's

---

[18] Cars in Ireland are driven on the left side of the road, not the right, as we do in the United States.

doorstep after a hard day's run. They looked like they were Basset Hounds. I knew I was going to like this place. My kind of town, Eignough is!

Steve and Peggy lived in a duplex—a house attached on one side to another house—on Hennessey Road. It was laid out almost like our place. No wonder they felt so much at home with us, with all the rooms in approximately the same place and all.

When we arrived, Peggy had already laid the dining room table for supper. I wasn't quite ready for eating just yet—I was already having a hard time getting use to the time difference, it being five hours later here than back home. I wanted a walk first, and then a long nap. I began sniffing around for a suitable door to stand next to—my signal for "gotta go, now". I made it to the front door, where we first came in, and Mom took me out again.

When I came back, I saw Lucie napping on her blanket on the heath, warming her back by the small fire.

She was just as Steve described her, with golden, amber eyes and a mostly brown coat that covered all of her slender body. Her white markings were so similar to mine, we could have passed for twins. She was a bit smaller than I, but a Basset Hound just the same. I ambled over to sniff her nose and was greeted with a warm lick on my jowl. We were instant friends. I whimpered "Hello"; she whimpered back, and I settled in on the hearth next to her to enjoy a cozy nap before dinner.

I must have been really tired, because it wasn't until early the next morning that I woke up, hungry as anything. I had slept right through dinner! Bassets are, at heart, couch potatoes and love to sleep, but this was ridiculous. Mom called it "jet lag". I call it just being plain lazy.

Peggy took Lucie and me out to the large lot behind the house, which she called a "garden"—but it wasn't really a garden; there were no flowers or plants, as such—we call it a backyard—to do our "stuff" and to romp a bit in the grass. My favorite thing back home was to roll and stretch on my back on wet, newly mowed grass, and here I had all the wet, green sod I could handle. I rolled and rolled and wriggled on my back, waving my paws, all four of them, in the air in pure delight. The best thing was that the "garden" was bordered by a wooden slat fence and we could roam around it at will without having to be on a leash, like back home, where every time I had to go out, Mom had to accompany me.

Lucie and I could come and go as we pleased via a flapped hole in the back door that Peggy taught me how to use, coaxed on by a few liver treats. I had to go in and out several times, rewarded each time by those treats, to get use to using the door just right. After I had learned that nifty trick, Lucie and I could go out to the garden to run and play together anytime we wanted.

What a concept! What a sense of freedom! I'm loving this place already!

As I mentioned before, Eignough is on the mouth of the River Shannon, with its own marina and small shipping port. On the afternoon of my first day there, Mom walked me down Francis Street to the marina, where she pointed out in the far distance, across the waters, a small, deserted island. The stroll took us a half hour or so and I was glad of the one-on-one time with her after such a long plane flight and nap. I love my Mom and cherish the times we can be together. So often, she is so engrossed in her work or writing that she forgets me pining away on the couch or sprawled out by her feet while she slaves at her desk at home. Maybe on this trip, I hoped, we could make up for lost time.

We found an expanse of cropped crab grass along the shore and Mom—wishes do come true—took a tennis ball out of her jacket pocket and rubbed it against my nose. It smelled of stale liver treats, and a few biscuit crumbs stuck to it.

"Here, boy," she teased. "Wanna play? Play fetch?" She tossed the ball across the field, expecting me to chase after it and bring it back to her. Ha! Easier said than done, even if it did smell like liver.

Now, I am a Basset Hound and my breed does not fetch; at least none of my kind that I know of do. We are hunters. We sniff out rabbits, birds, squirrels, and sometimes foxes, and point them out to our masters. We do not retrieve. I gladly leave that to the Goldens and Labradors and Jack Russells of our canine kingdom. Fetch? You have got to be kidding. Okay, maybe once or twice as a puppy I did bring the proverbial tennis ball back to Mom when she threw it down the main hallway of our house, but that was all. Much to her chagrin, I wasn't going to belie the innate characteristic of a Basset's inner nature. I repeat: we do not fetch.

But, after all, I reasoned, it *was* Ireland, where anything could happen, right? And, we were on a holiday together and this *was* the first time in a long time Mom expressed a desire to play with me for an extended period of time. So, I ran after the ball, found it behind a rock near the water, and stood there with my forepaw holding it down, proudly looking at her as if I had discovered the Hope Diamond in a sand dune. She stood expectantly at the edge of the field, waiting for me to return with the ball. I stood at attention over it, waiting for her to come get it, and voraciously praise me for finally playing the game.

She stood for awhile, with that disappointed-in-me look mixed with incredulity that she sometimes has when she thinks I've done something wrong or unexpected.

"Woof! What?" I barked. "Come and get me and this silly ball!"

Finally, she stomped over to me, picked up the ball and put it back into her pocket. I, on the other hand, found a long stick and offered it to her to play tug-tug. If nothing else besides eating and sniffing and sleeping, I was a champion tug-tug player. And so, we pulled and tugged at the stick together for the next hour or so. It and my antics made Mom laugh; it amazes me how such a simple game makes her so happy.

When we returned to the duplex, Steve had the plans to Castle Keep spread out on the dining room table. They spilled off onto a chair and the floor. He was studying them intently, making notes here and there, while Peggy scrutinized the copy of Vincent's father's will. She got up to make tea for Mom, gave me a gravy biscuit, and then settled in for a serious discussion.

"We have to personally prove in court who we say we are," she said, making notes on a beige writing tablet with a fountain pen. "Did you happen to bring a copy of your birth certificate along with your passport, June?" she asked Mom.

"Yes, and print-outs of the genealogy tree and supporting documents from the research I did on the Internet. They're all upstairs in my carry-all."

"Great!" Peggy said. "Steve and I have ours. Then all we need to do is to go to the courthouse in Ennis, file for release of the title in our names, and we're in business."

"What about Rick, my brother?"

"I will pay him his share out of the profits of the sales of Castle Keep units," Steve said, not raising his head bowed over the plans. "I think he'd be fine with a percentage, and then, later on, we can put his name on the deed to the McInerney castle."

"Deed? Castle?" Mom asked. "Do you mean we're going to keep it?"

"Yes. We'll hold it in reserve for ourselves. I talked it over with Peggy," he said, "and she had the interesting idea of perhaps turning it into a bed and breakfast, or some sort of tourist attraction. Out-of-towners that visit County Clare would like that sort of thing."

"We'll make it really authentic, with medieval coats of armor, and flags of various Irish tribes," Peggy added. "Not to mention the food—rashers and eggs[19], Irish stew, tea and wheat cakes, and, of course, Mock Goose."

"Whooo-hooooo!" I howled. I was hoping they'd let hounds stay in the new bed and breakfast. That would be awesome.

---

[19] A kind of bacon that is 99% meat, 1% fat. Eggs are typically served "over well".

"How about we add a small kennel so that guests can bring their dogs?" Mom asked, almost as of she had read my mind. Well, of course she did.

"Grand idea," Steve said. "I'll add the crèche to the plans."

By the end of our first week in Eignough, Ireland, the humans had gone to Ennis to file for probate and settlement of the will, and Steve had offered his plans to the planning offices of both Eignough and County Clare for approval to construct Castle Keep. Via email on Mom's laptop—she is never without it—my "uncle" Rick agreed to take a percentage of the profits provided he retained a partial share in the castle. Everything seemed to be settled except, of course, for the waiting.

"It might take some time," Steve explained. "Or not."

While we waited, the humans spent part of their time finalizing plans, while Lucie and I romped in the garden and snoozed together by the open fire in the hearth. It turned out, she was very adept at tug-tug, too. So we played for hours, pulling a thick length of rags twisted together between us.

One day, Steve borrowed a "pick-um-me-up" truck from his construction company, MacErignough and Dawes. With me and Lucie riding in the truck bed, and the humans crammed three abreast in the cab, we toured the countryside.

First, we drove up N67 to the Cliffs of Moher. I wasn't so anxious this time with Steve driving, as I now know the left side of the road was here, in Ireland, the right side. The cliffs rise at Hag's Head over the Atlantic Ocean. Lucie and I reveled in smelling the clean, salty air and having the sea breezes lift the velveteen flaps of our ears up as we raced up and down the mossy tundra high above overlooking the seas. Then we headed inland to Aillwee[20] Cave, which is part of a system of passages over a kilometer[21] long that leads under the Burren Mountain.

Mom read the plaque which said that the cave was discovered in 1944 by a farmer named Jacko McGann who followed his dog who chased a rabbit into the hole. I'd bet anything that that dog was a Basset Hound! Mom, Steve, and Peggy took the circular tour to see the waterfall, the stalactites and stalagmites, the

[20] This means "yellow cliff".
[21] A unit of length equal to 1,000 metres or 0.62 miles.

paintings, and the remains of bears—apparently it was a bear den at one time—while Lucie and I stayed outside snoozing in the sunshine on two of Peg's old quilts in the back of the truck.

On the way back on N18, we stopped to have a very late lunch in a restaurant in a hotel that was reconstructed in the shell of an old castle. There, believe it or not, the owners let Lucie and I, if we were well-behaved, sit and eat by our mistresses' sides while they dined; but only if we were good, which we were. We were too tired from the day's adventures to do anything else but! The waiter even provided us with our own china bowls to eat our most delicious corned beef and cabbage and drink cool, spring water. I relished the beef and potatoes, but left the cabbage. It didn't quite smell right for eating. Yuck! The hotel was a bit too posh for my taste—I am used to early American Basset décor, myself. However, it did provide Peggy and Mom with lots of ideas on how to restore the McInerney Castle, and what to do and not to do to please the tourist crowd.

We got home really late that night. I was drained of energy. All I could do was to use the garden and then crawl into bed next to Mom. Our room was on the third floor of the townhome and she had to practically carry me up the last flight of stairs. Touring Ireland is really wonderful, but very exhausting!

The next morning over breakfast, consisting of rashers and eggs over easy with tomatoes and wheat cakes for the humans and kibble splashed with gravy for Lucie and I, Peggy began opening the previous day's mail. Excuse me, since we're in Ireland, she began opening the post.

"A letter from the probate court in Ennis," Peggy said, opening and reading it. "We're in! They've processed the will and now we are the sole heirs of Vincent McInerney, Sr.! Praise be!"

We all cheered and howled and Lucie did a little dainty dance around the table, which I thought a bit too undignified for a Basset, but didn't bark anything as she looked so cute doing it, her long ears flapping over her shoulders. During her dance, the phone, er, telly rang in the hallway. Steve went to pick it up and after a while came back with what I would call a "beef-eating" grin on his face. If he wasn't so human, I would have thought he was a Basset Hound in disguise.

"We're in! The zoning board approved our plans," he said, smiling from ear to ear and hugging Peggy and Mom, each in turn. "We can break ground next week!"

Again, we all cheered and howled and, of course, all joined Lucie in her little dance. Everything was turning out just the way we expected and wanted it to. Life was indeed brilliant, er, grand in Ireland!

That morning to celebrate, after Mom and I cleaned up the breakfast dishes—I got to lick them clean, just as I do back home—just call me "pre-wash"—Peggy and Steve drove us down to the marina in the "pick-um-me-up" truck, where we rented a large rowboat, called a curach. We sailed, um, rather Steve and Peggy rowed us out to the small, deserted island that Mom and I saw on our first full day when she attempted to play "fetch" with me on the expanse of crab grass.

It was a little dicey getting used to the movement of the boat, the small waves of the River of Shannon lapping at its sides. Lucie seemed to be more adept, having, she explained later, been on a boat with her humans "lots of times". She had even learned how to swim! Fancy that! Bassets are not known to be swimmers, although a few of us have taken a liking to the water. The last time I tried it at Wagsworth, I nearly sank to the bottom of that salinated pool if it were not for the big life-preserver they put on me with the long lunge line attached to it to guide my paddling to the steps in the shallow end so far away. When I realized both Lucie and I were in a small boat in the middle of the river with no such safeguard, I began to panic.

"Easy, big fella," Mom said, trying to calm me down and soothe my nerves as my whole body shook and shivered to the very large, white tip of my tail. So much so, that the whole boat swayed from side to side. When Bassets get scared, we *really* get scared.

"Nothing to it. We're not going to sink and, if we do, I'll help you to swim ashore," Mom said. These were comforting words, indeed, coming from a human who grew up on the shores of the Hudson River and had learned to swim and sail at a very early age—doing so just about every summer day of her life! What chance had I, a land-bound Basset, with the build of a bull, in the middle of the veritable ocean if we hit, what? An iceberg?

"Woof! Please don't rock the boat in these waters, FrankieB," Lucie said. "Relax. I've done this a dozen times. Nothing is going to happen."

And nothing did. After a while, with a somewhat calmer me cowering in the stern with my nose on the transom, looking warily at the water and the safe shore we had left behind, we did arrive safely.

On the island, we discovered lots of grass to roll in, a beach to run on, and a courtyard to explore. Peggy had brought a picnic basket full of goodies for lunch and spread a plaid tablecloth on the ground next to the entrance of the courtyard.

Lucie and I ventured in through the wrought-iron gates, followed by our humans. We found a small, stone marker in the midst of large flagstones, which looked like a tombstone. But, Mom said, based upon the history she had been reading about the area, that that couldn't be the case. It was probably just that—a marker. Our humans, while Lucie and I sniffed around the courtyard, couldn't read the inscription, it being in Gaelic and all. Although they are true-blue, er, true-green Irish, Peggy and Steve had never really learned their native language, only smatterings of trite and common phrases. However, they did promise to have a proper translation of the inscription ready by the time Mom and I returned.

"Returned?" I barked. "Woof, howl-oooo-ooowl-oooowl! You mean we're coming back?"

But that meant we, Mom and I, would have to leave. That is, to go back "home". Mom patted my head in agreement. I suddenly felt very sad, because I thought this place, this wonderfully unique, green spot in Ireland, with Peggy and Steve and Lucie, was going to be our *new* home.

"Even so, FrankieBernard," Mom said, "we do need to go back. There are a few things I need to take care of. It's not our home, at least not for now, but, maybe, someday, it might be. For now, we have to go back to the States. I have to finalize my early retirement and make plans for our future. You do understand, don't you, big guy?" she asked, cradling my head in her arms.

"Sure," I woofed, muffling into the sleeves of her sweater. "Sure."

How I hated the thought of leaving my new best friend, Lucie, and Peggy and Steve...

With all our activities, time passed all too quickly, and, finally, it was the last few days of our last week In Eignough.

The day before we left, MacErignough and Dawes held a groundbreaking ceremony on the tract of land that was to become the Castle Keep development.

In front of the ruins of the old McInerney Castle, Steve's crew had propped up a large canvas green and white striped canopy. Under it, they set up round tables and chairs, and a long dais where the Mayor of Eignough sat alongside Steve, Peggy, and Mom. Lucie and I lay at their feet under the tablecloth, our wet noses peeking out from under the hem to watch the crowd of workers and townspeople gather on the grounds and under the tent.

There were balloons flying everywhere and green and white streamers adorned the big caterpillar bulldozers and mechanical shovels that were parked alongside the tent. A big sign graced the entrance:

CASTLE KEEP

a new MacEignough and Dawes Community,

that was draped in the Irish green, white, and orange flag.

Steve and the mayor both made speeches about how this new development community would do wonders for the town and how the restoration of the McInerney Castle would be a boon to the tourist trade, which made up the major portion of the area's industries. Then, quite by surprise, Steve handed Mom a silver-grey shovel with a red ribbon tied on its shaft and escorted her to a roped-off area in front of the tent.

"As our American cousin, and cherished guest of honor," he said, "please start the hole for the foundation of the first row of townhomes to be built at Castle Keep."

Mom was thrilled and, while the shovel was a bit too big for her to handle, she managed to stab the blade into the ground and stomp on it with her foot, shod in a very stylish, low-heeled boot. Lucie and I scrambled out from under our hiding place and began pawing at the cut Mom made to help her make the hole bigger. Bassets are also great diggers—just ask Mom about how I dig up all the peanuts that the squirrels bury in our backyard back home.

The crowd cheered and clapped and the mayor gave Mom a hug. Steve and Peggy gave both Lucie and I liver treats and vigorously patted our backs.

After the ceremony, three families from outside Eignough, without even looking at the floor plans, gave Steve large deposits for each of the bigger, four bedroom, three-and-a-half-bath townhouses, with finished basement, two wood-burning fireplaces, and a two-car garage.

We were in business!

That night for supper we celebrated with a special surprise dish that Peggy made in secret the day before for all of us, Bassets and humans alike—Mock Goose! It was delicious—I had never had such a glorious meal as that in all my life. Never! And to think I'd have it again for Christmas!

It certainly was a brilliant, er, grand day.

But, sadly, the next day had to come and come it did.

Early that morning, Steve loaded our luggage into the boot of his car and after many lingering good-byes and pets and belly rubs from the humans, and sniffing of noses and neck hugs between Lucie and myself, he drove Mom and me to Shannon International for the long flights home.

And so, I once again found myself back on a Pet Express jet, this time by myself. Sad though I felt, I was elated to be treated more royally by the stewards then on my first trip over. They must have sensed my loneliness as I dejectedly draped my nose and ears over my crossed paws, because they offered me many treats and scratches on my large occipital[22].

Mom took another big Aer Lingus A330 jet back home, this time flying in coach, which was still as plush or "posh", as Peggy would say, by our standards, as flying business class. Except, she had to sleep in a recliner seat and instead of her own assigned bed.

We both flew into New York's JFK International Airport and arrived in the early afternoon at about the same time. Mom rented a two-door Jeep Cherokee to drive us back to our home outside of Philadelphia. It was a great two and a half hours together, with me riding "shotgun" to navigate us around the big tractor-trailer "rigs", speeding along on the New Jersey Turnpike. Already, not yet home from our first trip, we were planning our second one back to Eignough, County Clare, Ireland!

Once home, the first thing we did after unloading our luggage was to fetch Sebastian. Well, actually, Mom went and got him. Remember, I do not "fetch". There was so much I wanted to tell him and, I had hoped, he

---

[22] The occipital is a small, wedge-shaped bone on top of the back of the head of a Basset Hound. It is said that the more pronounced the occipital, the brighter, smarter the hound.

had lots to tell me. But once home, he was so busy prowling around the house and snuggling in Mom's open suitcase on her, er, our bed to catch the smells of her and Ireland, that he fairly ignored me.

Oh, well, maybe next time.

The next day, bright and early, Mom turned in her resignation and sat down at her desk on the corner of the family room, with me and SabbyCat nestled in the couch for a nap while she "worked". This time, however, she started writing about and for us!

And that is how Mom became a full-time author, poet, and playwright, and how I and Sebastian became characters in this story; and how you came to be our dear readers.

PART III:

FRANKIE POETRY

These poems were written
over the course of many years,
mostly during the lifetime (16.5 human years)
that I owned "Frankie"
or, rather, that he "owned" me.
They apply equally well, and with just as much love,
to my current companion, "FrankieB".

They are published in
Spinach Water: A Collection of Poems,
by June J. McInerney,
and are reproduced here
for your delight and enjoyment.

For, after all, one cannot fail
to have the soul of a poet if one
has a Basset Hound for a friend.

FRANKIE POEM: I

the Battle of Tartars began
when Pinkstone raised
and grasping her opponent's lowered jaw
began scraping against his teeth
with the point of her weapon
digging into gum
hooked and peeled and pried
drawing blood dripping
through his open mouth over tongue
onto her silver colored shield.

He lunged at his attacker
teeth bared and snarling
to catch Pinkstone's hand
but she stepped back just in time
instead he caught mine
and realizing his mistake
whipped free of her grasp
flailing claws into the air
scratched my outstretched arm

My blood mingled with his own
on the shield top as
Pinkstone's enemy
scuttled off into a corner
whining retreat.

She stooped to further conquer
over his cowering form
making him lie lower
with a firm hand pressing down
the nape of his neck
until Frankie's snarling simpered
into silence.

On the drive home,
he nuzzled my neck
standing guard between bucket seats
faithfully watching for intruders
beyond the windshield.
It is his job to protect;

            the Battle was totally forgotten
a blemish on our history together
until that evening when
I inadvertently used a toothpick
in front of him
to clean my own teeth of dinner.

FRANKIE POEM: II

Species beyond boundaries,
languid, drooping gaze
catches always me up short.
Flews pressed against carpetry,
quiet look momentarily
of expectation,
"Play with me?"
Forever he'd lie lovingly
until I reach out to his toy
or caress ears crooning,
"Such a good boy!"

Brown eyes see beyond eternity,
knows of no mortality
only of now today.
Paws and stretches lazily
then romps away,
"Okay, I play?"
Stick, Frisbee. Toss, I catch
makes me laugh at
folding ears flapping happily.

I found him while buying cat food
scratching at his glass wall cage.
"Take me home, my name is Frankie,"
cuddled against my shoulder
quietly peed upon.

Here's no major decision,
just a quiet moment's hesitation
looking already fondly into his sad gaze.
A choice is made at a rare nexus
of one's life,
when you knew any other
would change both existences forever.

Dog Fancy

(Pour Sylvie, ma nouvelle amie,
qui rit de mes jeux de mots. Merci.)

I own a Basset,
(or does he own me?);
an around-the-town
tri-colored hound
with an attitude,
who gnaws on humorous bones
for amusement.

He pants the turn
of a verbal trick:
"Whaddya call a boomerang
that doesn't come back?"
"Stick."
And, bays at offering
a second ploy:
"Whaddya call a stick returned?"
"Dog toy."

FRANKIE POEM: III

Someday, in the future,
I'll have to put you down, and
lay your body rendered ashes
into the ground, perhaps in
an empty can of your favorite brand
of pet food, under the deck --
or do you think I'd leave you
at the vet, becoming anonymous,
like other pet parts in a pile?

I don't think so.

Because lately ,
I have come to believe
you will never leave.
Your body may go away,
but your spirit is mine.
Eternally, like today,
you'll howl and bay,
run and play,
flapping ears in the sun
greeting breezes, catching distant
scents of summer.
Your white tipped tail
will always be held aloft,
a flagpole of sorts,
proudly signaling
wherever you go, invisible
standards of innocence

We are friend and companion,
you know.
This is a forever bond,

never to be broken:
You, joyously glued to my side,
bounding, being.
Me, who'd never be without you,
knowing, caring.

We are forever one,
a soul.

RAVI'S POEM

(for Laura)

Little light tan eyebrows.
That's what caught me.
Condensed winter wooly bear
caterpillars on a hill of a face
soon broadening into a pitch black
mountain of time.

Rays of light glistening
in bright browns,
eager to learn, eager to please,
Ravi rescaled sun-filled face,
I see my life's days
rising and setting
in your eyes.

Foundling kennel-whipped
dirty on naked city streets,
Philly dog pup, I think not
suburban open fields for you,
but opened hearts to heal
your open wounds scarred already
from wandering battles
you have no words yet to tell;
but how you have related your tale
in the few short furry weeks
we've been together

getting to know you
in my home, testing me
in your heart. Long stretches on the
couch,
occasional snarls, a taste or two
of a friendly hound.
Even behind sunshine
clouds a little darkness.

You've even brought
a pet's pests to bear.
But, I don't mind.
You're mine.

THAT DOGGONE FEELING

Now,
I'm feeling
a little lighter,
a little taller,
slightly happier,
quieter,
more secure,
self-assured,
a little more relaxed,
with
a soupçon of delight
funding humor
in the universe
like a
housebound
Basset hound
finally freely sniffing
feral squirrel
in the woods.

ABOUT THE AUTHOR

June J. McInerney is an accomplished author, poet, and librettist. Her works include a book of spiritual inspirations; a variety of children's stories and musicals; and various slim volumes of poetry:

Meditations for New Members

Children's Stories (for all ages)
Adventures of Oreigh Ogglefont

Musicals
Written in collaboration with the composer, Linda F. Uzelac, who is also the illustrator of this book.
We Three Kings
Beauty and the Beast
Bethlehem
Noah's Rainbow
Peter, Wolf, and Red Riding Hood
All are available at www.stagedoormusicals.com

Poetry
Spinach Water
Exodus Ending

Originally from the New York metropolitan area, she currently lives near Valley Forge Park in Pennsylvania with her constant and loving companions, FrankieBernard and Sebastian Cat.

Please read the author's blog on her Web site:
www.JuneJMcInerney.com

Please visit the illustrator at her Web site:
www.stagedoormusicals.com

Made in the USA
Middletown, DE
14 February 2020

84171734R00142